SPIKED

RESORT TO MURDER BOOK 3

AVERY DANIELS

Blazing Sword
Publishing Ltd.

Avery Daniels/Blazing Sword Publishing, Ltd.

Colorado Springs, CO 80907

www.blazingswordpub.com

Book Layout & Design Vellum

© Cover Art, Layout, and Design by Jess Smith/InkblotsArt

SPIKED/ Avery Daniels. -- 1st ed.

ISBN 978-0-9990318-9-6

❀ Created with Vellum

*Dedicated to all the people in my life who
make this journey a little easier: friends who support and listen
through good and tough times
and fellow writers who plot with me and
nurture my writing. I couldn't do this without
each and every one of you.*

Special thanks to my Beta Reader Barbara Quigley.

.

"I believe that everybody has three lives, a public life, a private life, and a secret life."

—Meryl Streep

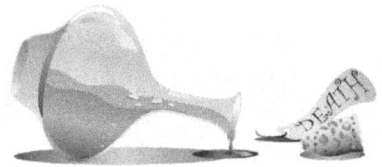

CHAPTER 1

"What do you mean you don't like weddings?"
My boss Chad asked with his hands on his hips. He was tall and lanky with sandy blonde hair and always had either an anxious or displeased look.

"I... um... " I was at a loss to explain why the thought of coordinating this large-scale rehearsal, dinner, wedding, and reception was more like a punishment than business as usual.

We stood inside the Colorado Springs Resort's elegant ballroom next to the black polished grand piano and surveyed the two thousand five hundred square feet. I love its thirty-five majestic fluted columns lining the walls and in a line up the center of the floor like identical floor-to-ceiling statues adorning the room. Twelve massive crystal chandeliers cast a golden glow over the linen-covered tables and marble floor.

"Doesn't every woman grow up planning every little detail from the age of five?" Chad cocked his blonde head to the side.

"Nooooo. At least I never did. Besides, haven't you ever heard of *The Bridezilla*? It's a nightmare creature come to life and will suck an event planner of her very life force." Okay, maybe it was a slight exaggeration, but not by much I feared.

I'm Julienne LaMere, resort management trainee at the Colorado Springs Resort, a sprawling complex of Italianate luxury originally built in 1918 and a member of the Historic Hotels of America.

You might have picked up on the fact that my love life was... pathetic. I broke up with two different men recently, and I was still a bit sad over the last one – my neighbor Mason.

I decided to just suck it up and plow through the assignment. Chad wouldn't understand anyway. "So I'll suggest Clasico Italiano for the rehearsal dinner and this for the wedding reception itself."

No woman wants to plan the happy day for another when she had ended two relationships in six months. I had my reasons to call it quits, and they were still good reasons.

But, planning a wedding was a knife in the heart. If I were given to romantic dreams of a wedding, which I'm not, I'd have the ceremony here. I'm a fan of marble columns and the decorative leaded windows. *Sigh.*

"Ariya will be here in a minute with the groom's father... and his checkbook, so let's get this pulled together. This is a big event and we need it after the murder last fall. Make it happen, last minute or not." Chad turned and walked out.

Sheesh. Touchy.

Last fall was the murder of a nationally prominent pastor during an event in our conference center. I was the prime suspect, so I dug up other likely killers for the police and our reputation was still recovering.

Then just a few short months ago I attended a Resort Management conference in Chad's place and helped solve a double homicide while snowed in at the ski resort. But it was springtime with flowers blooming and trees greening up and all was right with my world... except in the romance department.

I loved my job; it was my dream to manage resorts around the world and I've been fortunate to be trained in my hometown of Colorado Springs. I know how lucky I am to work in the luxury of the classic Mediterranean styled resort every day even if parts of the job aren't my favorite.

I had barely been alone a full minute when two men and a lovely young woman joined me. The older gentleman was balding, had a midlife paunch, was about five-foot-nine, and other than his obviously well tailored suit he was unremarkable.

My eyes couldn't help but gravitate towards the younger of the two men. He had movie-star good looks, those finely chiseled features that seem perfection, rich bronze skin, his black hair fell in short loose curls, stunning milk-chocolate brown eyes that looked directly at you and gave the impression he really saw you. He was dressed in light gray slacks and light blue polo shirt that made his skin glow. He was clearly related to the lovely young lady, sharing the perfected features, dark hair, and coloring.

The older gentleman reached his hand out, "Miss LaMere, I'm Landon Garrett this is my soon to be daughter-in-law Ariya, and her brother just in from England, Liam."

Ariya was the bride I needed to please, but Landon made it clear without saying a word that he felt I was working for him alone. Oh, this was going to be a joy. Then throw in the handsome brother and this next week promised to be more of a struggle. Handsome men were trouble. I knew from experience. Mason was equally handsome, but in a more rugged way than this polished Brit.

"I'm grateful for your accommodating us at the last moment. We had to rearrange the dates for my brother and father." Ariya had a voice reminiscent of a finely tuned violin, beautiful to listen to and expressive and with only a hint of a British accent. Her hands gracefully indicated the younger of the two men.

"Indeed, I'm the bloke who should express our thanks." The British brother's voice was rich milk-chocolate with a dash of chili powder for some heat. His direct gaze and wicked smile confirmed my first impression. Trouble, with a capitol T.

I turned on my resort professional persona, "This is our Grand Ballroom that I'm suggesting for the reception. We can accommodate a band and a piano player," I indicated the features with my hand, like a game show model. "We just had the Steinway baby grand tuned in anticipation of using it." The piano was glossy black and sat up on a slight dais where any musicians would be tucked away. They smiled appreciatively.

Mr. Garrett stepped up onto the dais and ran through the scales on the piano. "Exquisite sound," was his only comment.

"From here we can look at the venue next door for the wedding of your size, then make our way over to the restaurant I'm recommending for the rehearsal dinner."

They were incredibly lucky that we could fit a wedding of two hundred people so suddenly, but we had a cancellation of our own.

"Will any of your visitors or family be staying at the hotel?" If many of the wedding party were staying here, I wanted to make sure they got a complimentary basket in their rooms.

"My father, Liam, and my grandparents from India plus a few of Jason's out-of-state family as well will stay here." Ariya replied.

"If you can give me their names, I'll ensure they have a warm welcome on your behalf."

I showed them the space we had for the wedding ceremony and went over the decorating options. It was a large open space with custom plush carpet, massive cut crystal chandeliers, carved moldings and accents all in cream colors to match with any required event decorations. It smelled fresh as a result of the recent carpet cleaning after the last event.

"I think the platinum package is best," Mr. Garrett said to Ariya. "I'll discuss it with your father but I'm sure he'll agree with me." Clearly money must not be an issue. That package included the arched trellis, plush padded seating decorated in silk coverings with satin bows, thirty artificial trees strung with white lights, and the walls hung with gauze draped twinkle lights, plus the carpet down the center for the bridal procession.

Mr. Landon Garrett was surprisingly into the details as much as any mother I'd ever heard about.

"I took the liberty of having one of our chefs meet you to discuss the reception menu." I introduced them to Claude who turned on the charm for clients but was a tyrant to the rest of us.

They had a cake ordered already, but their prior wedding venue provided catering in-house like we insist upon. Normally, I would go over the options, but Claude didn't like the last minute addition, so I insisted he personally meet with the client. I knew he would never take his frustrations out on them.

I backed away for them to discuss options and leaned against a wall. I closed my eyes for a second, enjoying a few moments to myself.

"Mind if I join you?" Liam's chocolate decadence voice broke my peace. He leaned his shoulder against the wall next to me. His eyes fixed on my face.

"You don't want to talk entrees and desserts?" I kept my eyes on the bride, best not to look directly at Liam. His voice reminded me of the sultry midrange notes on my clarinet and I've always had a fondness for British accents. I was silently cursing the television and movies of my youth with their suave British actors stealing hearts.

"I'd fancy a chat with you. We honestly appreciate your fitting us in at the last minute and all. I was going to miss Ariya's wedding because of work, but she moved it forward to fit my schedule." He wasn't touching me, but his voice was so close it felt intimate.

Eyes forward, don't look. *Don't look, he'll suck you in.* "What is it you do Mr…?"

"Call me Liam, or Rajesh – my middle name, whichever you prefer. I'm in public relations for a very demanding organization."

I nodded my head as if his job was interesting, but didn't say another word.

"In case you're wondering, my Brit father picked my first name and my Indian mother my middle, they swapped for my sister."

I nodded my head again and kept my eyes on the bride.

"Do you have something against Indians?"

"Noooo. I'm just focused on my job."

"Did I do something to…?"

"You're fine Mr. Bryan," in more ways than one I said to myself. I wasn't going to use his first or middle name. *Strictly professional.* "But, I need to remain focused on the wedding and all its details to ensure we meet all expectations." Like I said, trouble.

I strolled back to the table where Chef Claude had catering menus and a few samples for Ariya and Mr. Garrett. Liam followed and stood next to me without touching me, but I could feel the heat from his body.

"Do you have a sugar-free cake option? My wife is diabetic, and she hates to miss out. Perhaps a small little personal sized cake for her?" Mr. Garrett had finished his sampling.

"Oh yes, we must accommodate Lillian." Ariya hurried to add.

Claude was most accommodating for the client as I knew he would be.

All told it was an hour later when they had all the catering decided.

We were on the west side of the property and our next stop was across the lake on the east side. I led them like a pied piper across the lake via a lovely wide walkway with stone sidings and smooth cement surface with a humped bridge insert at midpoint for swans and paddle boats to cross underneath freely.

I walked them to the Clasico Italiano restaurant, and they were pleased with the private room for their rehearsal dinner. Then I ushered them to the front steps of the hotel as we finished the meeting. I noticed a squirrelly guy paying a bit of interest in our little group.

"Here's the information on my florist and the musicians for both the wedding and reception." Ariya handed me a hand-written note.

"I'll call them right away and coordinate with them. If you have any questions, please call me."

We arranged for Ariya to come by in a few days to go over any more details and begin bringing the centerpieces she was making for the reception tables.

Mr. Garrett and Ariya walked down the steps toward the parking area across the street, but Liam tapped me on the shoulder. I turned and looked him in the eyes. *Mistake.* I was drawn into his nearly hypnotic eyes. Oh, he knew his effect on women, and he enjoyed it.

"Do you have a boyfriend, then?" His eyes bore into mine. This guy didn't give up easy. "Ah, let me guess. It's complicated. Then you can tell me about it over dinner."

"I'm not allowed to fraternize with the guests."

"Can you recommend another hotel?" He smiled bright.

"We're the best in town." I smiled.

"I'd rather be in lesser accommodations and have dinner with you."

"I couldn't let you cheat yourself out of the grand experience of staying here." I was never any good at chess and this was feeling like I was being maneuvered into a checkmate.

"But you would cheat me of the honor and delight of dinner with you? That is most uncharitable." His eyes shone with determination and flirtation.

"That is a big assumption on your part, I might be dull and too tired from work to delight even the slightest." I countered.

"Then allow me to delight you, give you a night to relax and enjoy yourself in my company." His smile never wavered. What was the danger after all? He was only here for about a week. *Oh, he was good, I was already starting to give in.*

"Call me later, but I'll probably have to work late." That would get him to move on and provide an excuse for later.

"I'm staying here, remember, so I'll find you. Six-ish." He inclined his head, it felt like he had given me a bow. Oh, the Brits did have their charm.

Mr. Liam Rajesh Bryan walked towards the newer hotel on the west side of the lake and I looked over my notes to give him time to move out of sight. *I was not watching him, really. Okay, maybe a little. It was a fine view. I can look.*

An aggressive voice startled me, "I'm looking for a person and was hoping you could tell me if he's staying here or has business here." A medium-built man with thinning salt-and-pepper hair and mustache stood next to me. It was the squirrelly guy that had paid us some attention.

"I'm not at liberty to share such information." I wasn't either, privacy laws and all that.

"The man's name is Marks or probably something like that?" He was determined, but not in a charming way like Liam. I sensed he was stubborn and might become a nuisance.

He then pressed a twenty-dollar bill into my palm. I raised an eyebrow and handed it back with my best *how dare you insult me with a bribe* look.

"I can neither confirm nor deny such a person has anything to do with the resort. Now if you'll excuse me." I walked away, but when I glanced over my shoulder, he was jogging toward the parking lot.

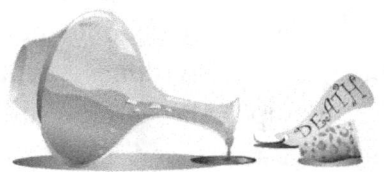

CHAPTER 2

*W*hen the resort was initially built the premier golf course architect of the day was hired to design the first course which became the highest golf course of the time. Over the years two more golf courses were added. Every major golf celebrity has played its links. This would be the second time we hosted a Ladies Professional Golf Association tournament. I was looking forward to getting some autographs and even considered taking some lessons myself.

I was deep in the middle of phone calls for the upcoming LPGA golf tournament in July when Liam, Landon Garret, and a young man I hadn't met yet entered my office. That was a surprise, I never told them where my office was and usually I met clients on the grounds since my office was tiny. I rushed to get off the phone.

"Ms. LaMere, this is my son Jason, the groom. While Ariya is at a final dress fitting I wanted to show Jason the arrangements if it's not too much trouble?"

I really wish they would have called and arranged a time, I was expecting several return calls about what Lady golfer's names we could feature on the promotional materials. Besides, I would have dressed nicer than the blush cotton blouse and pale grey pencil skirt.

"I can spare a few moments only, not many grooms are hands on with the wedding preparations, so I wouldn't want to dampen the enthusiasm." I plastered a smile on my face.

I was speed walking them over the lake's walkway, figuring the men could keep up, when Liam jogged up beside me.

"You skipped out on our dinner last night. I'm suffering from the blow to my self esteem." But his smile said otherwise. Today he wore a button-down shirt in a mint green and tan dress slacks that looked good on him.

"I don't think any permanent damage has been done, even to your ego. I suspect you'll live."

"Thank you for the complimentary welcome basket of local goodies. I had hoped for a personal note from you, but it was the pre-printed greeting." His voice had taken on a wounded tone.

I got the trio of men to the wedding venue in my personal fastest time and did the game-show girl routine again. It was in the grand ballroom for the reception where the Garrett men left me alone with Liam while they visited the gentleman's restroom.

If Landen Garrett weren't the epitome of a stuffed shirt, I'd think this whole visit was a ruse to give Liam another opportunity.

"How about lunch at least? Lunch is casual, nonthreatening. We can even do one of those… food trucks I hear about." The gleam in his eye was fading, and he seemed more sincere. Should I take pity on the poor handsome Brit? *International relations training…?*

"Tell you what, I have some important calls yet to make. I was planning on eating at my desk, but if I get through my calls, I'll take you to a food truck."

"That wasn't so hard was it?" The wicked smile was back. "You might even enjoy my company."

"Whoa there mister, don't get carried away. It was rather difficult, actually." I smiled to soften the words. "And the jury is out on the quality of your company." *Was I flirting back or just picking on the self-assured hunk?*

Just when I was beginning to think father and son were taking a rather long bathroom break, they returned to the ballroom. Mr. Garrett was on his cell phone talking to what sounded like his job.

When we were out in the sunshine again, I hustled the men to wedding space and the restaurant for the rehearsal dinner. I thought I glimpsed the squirrelly man from yesterday walking the opposite direction, but I couldn't be sure.

I was finally done with the quick tour for the groom's sake and they went their way. I returned to my desk and waded back into the Ladies Pro Golf world again. I had missed two return calls.

Hours later I had made good progress and had a mockup for the promotional posters created on my computer, with a few big names to draw crowds. I sent my finished product in an email to Chad for his comments, and he always has comments.

Eleven-thirty, right about time for Liam to check in about the food truck run. I was considering offering to pick up something for Chad when my doorway was filled with… Detective Lawrence, the man who believed I had killed a celebrity pastor last fall. I had hoped to never see his face again in my lifetime.

I folded my arms and stared. That was the best I was giving him. That was taking a fair bit of restraint too, let me tell you.

"Ah Miss LaMere, we meet again. You appear well." He wore the same stern expression I remembered. He was dressed in a lightweight suit, no tie, his graying hair brushed back and perfect, and his muddy brown eyes evaluating me.

"I have nothing to say to you, Detective." I spoke louder than necessary so Chad could hear in his office. Within seconds Chad's head poked out from his doorway, anxious look in full force, and then the rest of him followed.

"Detective Lawrence, please tell me you stopped for a nice lunch or a stroll around the lake and nothing more." Chad's voice was already bordering on panic.

"Well, I have a suspicious death that you might be able to help me with." His gaze bounced between Chad and I.

At just that moment Liam joined the group, talk about terrible timing. I couldn't let Chad know I was running out for lunch with a hotel guest, it was against the strict policy.

Chad and the detective stopped and stared at Liam. Chad raised an eyebrow in my direction

"Mr. Bryan is… ah… part of the…" My mind was blank. *Busted.*

"Pardon me gentlemen, I'm in the Garrett/Bryan wedding and Ms. LaMere was going to assist me in finding where I'm to get a fitting for my tux."

Detective Lawrence gave me a pointed look that he didn't buy that cover story for a minute. Chad changed to accommodating at the mention of the last minute wedding I was to ensure was perfection itself.

"Detective, Julienne is busy. Perhaps I can be of assistance?"

"No, I need to know why Julienne's name was on a hotel card in the pocket of a man who died of what I am guessing was poison just a few hours ago. Amazing how you're connected with another death." His beady little eyes watched me. Well, they were menacing beady eyes to me in any case.

I could feel the blood drain to my toes. *Not again.*

Then the most unexpected thing happened, Liam took out his wallet and showed his identification to the Detective, who then stiffened and cleared his throat. I couldn't see what it said, but I sure as blazes wanted to know.

"I would fancy hearing about this death, for I'm sure that Ms. LaMere couldn't possibly be involved. But I would feel better knowing if there is any connection to my presence." He glanced my way and winked.

The Detective looked… nervous and Chad could catch hummingbird's with his mouth gaping open.

"Yes sir, or is it agent? We were called to a car crash just down the street," his thumb pointed toward Dream

Lake Drive, "when the man who had rear-ended a car and caused a chain reaction of fender benders was discovered dead." He checked his notes. "The Medical Examiner's preliminary COD is a cardiac arrest but the fact that he was vomiting in his car prior suggests perhaps a poison of some sort was involved. When I found *her* name I hoped she could tell me about him."

A stranger dies and he can't wait to talk to me. Gee, how did I ever get so blessed?

He flashed a photo from his phone of the dead man's driver's license in my face. "How do you know him?"

Roderick Rogers was the name on the license but I had to squint at the really bad photo on the ID.

"Oh, him. He was around yesterday looking for some-body named… oh let me think… um, Marks. Mr. Marks, I think. That was the one and only time I've spoken to him and I didn't give him a card."

"Who is this Mr. Marks?"

"I haven't any idea. I never heard of a Mr. Marks and I can't divulge information on our guests to unofficial personnel, anyway." I huffed.

"Did he say why he was looking for Mr. Marks?"

"No, he didn't. It was a very brief exchange."

The Detective looked at Liam, "Well, if I have any further questions I'll be in touch." He nodded to Liam.

At some point Chad had closed his mouth, but he continued to look at Liam from the corner of his eyes.

Once the Detective was out of earshot, I turned to Chad, "I'm going to assist Mr. Byran with locating a fitting for that tux of his. So many fine little details in this wedding and I must keep on top of them."

I grabbed my purse, locked my office, and snaked my arm through Liam's and made an exit as quickly as I could drag him away. Once we were outside and away from eager ears, I spun him around.

"Who are you? What was it you showed my nemesis the police detective that made him so nervous?" Because that was a cool trick and I wish I could make him nervous.

Liam's smile was soft. "Oh bugger. It'll spoil everything. Either women like what they think my job is about or are repelled." He slid his wallet from his back pocket and showed me… NO, it couldn't be.

I stared up at him doing an impression of Chad with my mouth open.

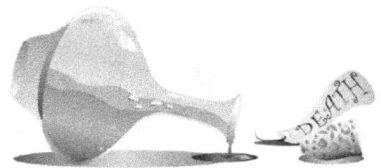

CHAPTER 3

"You're MI5? You said you worked in Public Relations. You're a spy, a spook, a covert operative? Oh, no… you're a Bond, a James Bond. This is so ironic." I wasn't overreacting, it really was ironic.

When I first met Mason, the last boyfriend that I recently broke up with, I had nicknamed him Bond Jr. My ringtone for him was even the theme from the last Bond movie. He had all the makings of a men's channel fantasy come to life. He appeared to be a playboy and takes bodyguard jobs with models and Hollywood actresses posing as their latest boy-toy. He even plays high stakes poker tournaments and is a martial arts expert. But the posing as other women's boyfriend was the dealbreaker for me, even if he was doing bodyguard work. He was the image of a Bond character.

Mason swore to me he wanted to have a serious relationship, no more Don Juan act. But he kept taking bodyguard jobs were he posed as their latest affair, and I cut him loose. Call me old-fashioned, naïve, prudish, close-minded, whatever but any man of mine can't be posing as somebody else's boyfriend.

Then this suave British dreamboat walks into my life and he actually is an agent for Her Majesty's Secret Service. *The universe had a warped sense of humor.*

"I'm not a covert operative, and I *am* in public relations. I'm one of a handful of people who provide a public face for the agency, so I'll never do covert missions," He looked at me with a touch of concern. "So, I take it you're the type who doesn't like what I do?"

I squirmed, "Well, it's more the persona. I don't like the Casanova type that spies bring to mind. Let's face it, you…" I gave him the slow scan from head-to-toe, "are the epitome of just that image."

He let out a huff of breath and blushed a bit which was adorable. "In reality, spies are very average so they fit in and go unnoticed," he ran a hand through his hair and mussed it up. "I'll admit I enjoy flirting but I actually don't date much since my job is very demanding of my time. In my teen years I couldn't get a date because I'm part Hindu Indian. For the record, I was raised with traditional values by both heritages. I simply wanted to enjoy the company of a lovely lady while on holiday."

Now I was blushing. But, I couldn't quite believe he didn't date "much" with his looks. He'd have women throwing themselves at him, he didn't need to actually date without having company anytime he wanted, day or night.

"Look, I am really peckish so if we could please eat…" His eyes implored.

I knew that one of the best food trucks would be only a few short miles from the resort today, and I had driven to work rather than walk the few blocks, so I was able to chauffeur. It felt strange having a British agent in my car, so I tried not to think about it.

We ordered and walked to the nearby park. The lawn was mostly greened up and smelled freshly mown. We sat across from each other on a small picnic table enjoying our food under some trees with a view of the green lawns stretching before us. I had the Gruyere Mac and Cheese and he got two deluxe Chili Cheese Dogs.

"How was your lunch?" I had waited until he finished eating.

"They weren't scrummy," at my confused look he clarified, "meaning they weren't delicious but they do have a certain appeal."

"I hear that England isn't known for its culinary delights, so consider this broadening your palate." I shot back.

He smiled, "Consider my palate dually broadened." He gazed around for a few moments and watched three noisy kids flying a kite and a man tossing a Frisbee for his dog to catch. "So, this bloke you saw yesterday that may have gotten murdered, tell me about him."

"Nothing remarkable. I saw him as I was showing your sister around and then he came up to me and said he was looking for a Mr. Marks. I told him I couldn't share that kind of information. But here's the thing, I'm not aware of a Mr. Marks. I didn't give him a card, I don't think I even told him my name. So I don't know what's going on." I was getting flustered.

"Why would the detective come to see you so soon?"

"Well, there was a murder last fall…" I told him about the murder and how I was the prime suspect.

"You're telling me you kneed the grabby drunk pastor, he gets murdered, and then you had to do your own investigation to clear your name?" He had a reserved smile and his voice dropped a register, "you surprise me, and that doesn't happen often in my world."

I couldn't look him in the eyes so I took out my phone and looked up any news of the accident on our local news social media and website.

After a few minutes I found what I was looking for, "Here we go. News report says Roderick (Rick) Rogers was the cause of a multiple car accident, blah, blah, blah, he was a local private detective." I scanned through the short notice. "It says he was in the running to have a reality show follow his exploits."

"Makes me wonder if he was investigating this Mr. Marks." Liam added.

"My thoughts exactly." I glanced at my watch, "I really must get back or I'll be in trouble."

We hustled to the car and made it back in quick time.

At the entrance to the hotel, Liam took my hand. "Now that I've demonstrated I'm not like the infamous Pastor you kneed in the bullocks, would you join me for dinner?"

Just my luck, at that very moment Mason, looking particularly handsome in tan slacks and a peach polo shirt that showed off his muscles, burst through the door of the hotel.

"There you are Julie…" He came to an abrupt halt,

glanced between Liam and me, saw our hands joined, and swallowed hard before saying, "I see you're busy, I'll talk to you later." He turned around and retreated back into the hotel.

My stomach sank as if I were cheating on him and just got caught. *Geez, LaMere. You haven't been together for the last three months.*

"Oh, crap." Slipped out of my mouth and I covered it with my free hand.

Mason would stop by my office about once a week with an excuse to chat. It was contrived since he lived across the street from my townhome. To say he was trying to win me back wasn't accurate, more like anticipating I would forget about everything. But, he still thought I just overreacted to his posing as other women's boyfriend for his bodyguard jobs and I needed to change, so no deal.

"Am I to gather he's a boyfriend?" Liam, in perfect British-stiff-upper-lip manner murmured while his face went blank of any emotion. Even for a movie-star-good-looking man like Liam, having Mason as competition couldn't be an easy pill to swallow… and vice versa.

"Former boyfriend. Recently split by a few months." I just admitted my pathetic status to a relative stranger, what was I thinking? I became aware of the people coming and going around us as we stood at the front of the hotel. I felt like I had bared my heartache to the whole resort.

He cleared his throat, "Let me be blunt. I fear you'll begin looking into the recently deceased Rick Rogers," his eyes narrowed, and he leaned toward me, "I want to assist you." He held up his hand to stop my objections before I could start them. "I've been involved in investigations in my *employment* and I'm trained, even though I don't do covert operations. I could help resolve this much faster." His British accent made it sound so logical.

He said the magic words, he could make this whole thing go away faster. Perhaps police information would be shared with him so I wasn't covering old ground. Plus, Detective Lawrence lost some of his nastiness in his presence.

Although I felt bad about Mason getting the wrong idea, I was tempted to take Liam up on his offer. There was a little devil on one shoulder telling me it would do Mason good to see me moving on. But, it would be a lie because I still held out hope he would come to his senses and we could get back together.

"I'll admit finding out what the deceased PI was working on had crossed my mind. I suppose you might be of assistance." I acquiesced.

"Good, we can discuss our strategy over dinner. My treat." His eyes looked hopeful, his smile was ever-so-slightly cocky.

"I have to go home when I'm done for the day here and get some things taken care of there. I'll return to my office around eight and we can strategize then. In the meantime, maybe you could begin preliminary research?"

"You are determined to thwart my dinner plans. So be it. I brought a laptop and power converter, I'll do some research on the dearly departed. See you eightish." He again bent forward slightly in a subtle little bow.

I just sat down at my desk when Chad poked his head out of his office, "I need to talk to you, come in."

Oh dear, did he realize I had a personal lunch with one of the guests? I tried to keep calm as I sat in the visitor chair on the other side of his desk. I squirmed and began twirling the pearl ring my father gave me on my sweet sixteenth birthday.

"It seems you have developed a rapport with Ariya's brother," he lowered his voice, "*the MI5 agent.* That could be to our advantage."

I kept my mouth shut, but I'm pretty sure that my eyes were about to pop right out of my head. What was he up to?

"I'm not sure I understand what you mean." I crossed my fingers this wasn't about lunch and held my breath.

"I was thinking with your experience investigating to clear your name last fall and then helping solve the murders in Vail a few months ago, you could help clear the hotel of any connection to this murder. Our reputation can't withstand any taint of scandal again." He paused and seemed to weigh his next words, "And if this agent would assist you... which I suspect he might be open to, so you can quickly get us cleared. He seemed to come to your defense fast." He stroked his five o'clock shadow, "I can't make this an official job duty, but I'd consider it above and beyond."

I translated this to mean I was to work my regular job and investigate on my own time without overtime pay. *Gee, what a deal.*

But I was going to investigate anyway, only now I could legitimately be in Liam's company without getting in trouble. That was at least one less thing to worry about.

"Will you get the surveillance tapes from Security for

the last five days for me?" We only had a few cameras around the property, but it might give me an idea of what Rick Rogers was doing around the resort.

"If that's a yes, I'll get those recordings to you pronto."

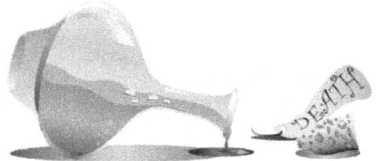

CHAPTER 4

I drove home at the end of the day wishing I could blow off the investigation and enjoy my evening. I had some flowers I wanted to plant. We wait until after Mother's Day to do much planting since we can still get some overnight freezing into mid-spring. My clarinet was beckoning me too. I rarely went a few days without playing, it helped me relax and think.

I grabbed my mailbox keys and walked out my front door, down my three steps and made my way to the community mailboxes in the center of the complex under some shade trees.

I scrutinized Mason's townhome across the street. He was home because Roulette, his Sheltie dog, wasn't at the window waiting dutifully for him, but he apparently didn't want to talk to me after seeing Liam hold my hand. I couldn't tell him that Liam didn't send jolts of electricity zinging through me like he did. *Sigh.*

I took my time at the mailboxes, hanging around to gossip with my neighbors. I lived in Mountain Shadows, a townhome complex with roughly eighty some units, a nice clubhouse that had a large meeting space with a couch, comfy chairs, table, full kitchen, plus the pool table, exercise equipment, and a Jacuzzi. The complex had a nice swimming pool and tennis courts too. It also had more than average share of "mature" homeowners.

Some of my favorite neighbors were zany, but good at helping me with the word on the street, or rather the garter belt gossip mill. I refer to them as my Resort Irregulars in honor of Sherlock Holmes' method of using people to gather information.

Beverly and Delores finally wandered over. Beverly was short like a fireplug with dark copper hair, tattoos, coordinated clothes and jewelry, and a snarly attitude where Delores was thin and taller with birdlike mannerisms, short cropped hair and plucked eyebrows. She wore more casual clothes and had a more pious outlook. They both drank wine by the gallon and could drink me under the table without trying, which is saying something since I grew up in a wine enthusiast family.

"Hey, we saw you hanging out, in the middle of the day no less. Figured you had something to share. What's up?" Delores cut to the chase. I must be interrupting a game show or something.

Clouds drifted over the sun and a breeze rattled the new leaves on the trees. I shivered in the cool air, I should have worn a sweater.

"Do either of you know of a local private investigator named Rick Rogers?" I just threw it out there not expecting much.

They looked at each other and then back at me,

"Sure, he's angling to get a reality show…" Delores began.

"Real Investigators or something like that." Beverly finished.

"It's him or this other local P.I., Mike Hammond, that'll be the Southwest's featured investigator." Delores jumped in.

"I like Hammond, he's better looking." Beverly's eyebrows danced a little jig.

"Mike Hammond, sounds like the old noir detective books… Mike Hammer wasn't it?" I asked. "Wonder if he changed his name or his parents had it in mind when naming him?

"I like the names being so close too. Of course, Hammond isn't as good looking as the actor who played Hammer in the old television show. Now he was hunky." Beverly obviously had thought on this a lot.

"Sure he's the better looking of the two, but I don't like Hammond as much, he's starting to get pretty cut-throat to win the competition to be on the reality show regularly. They ended up in a fistfight a few weeks back as they were trying to track the same person." Delores pursed her lips in disapproval and wrapped her sweater tighter around herself.

"Wow, they got into a fight? Was Rogers hurt badly?" This could be the killer.

"He got socked in the stomach pretty good. But he deserved it, he tried to cheat by paying for information." Beverly replied quickly.

"He wasn't cheating; he just understands you have to grease the wheels. Offering a free meal at a restaurant wasn't against the rules." Delores' face was turning red.

"Okay, guys. Enough. Is there anything that happened during the investigations? Can you think of anybody else that might have a grudge against him?" I tried to get them to focus.

They stopped arguing and looked at me.

"Why are you asking? Did something happen?" Beverly was the first to speak.

"You are suddenly interested in this competition. So what is it? Another murder? You can tell us dear." Delores winked.

They were bound to hear about it before very long if they were fans of this reality show. Besides, I wanted to get out of the chill air.

"I think he died in a car accident earlier." They would find out all the details through official channels soon. I wasn't a hundred percent sure he was poisoned, anyway.

Both of their mouths formed an "O" as they stared at me in surprise. A gust of invigorating air blasted through and I began to shiver a bit.

"Do you think it was murder?" Beverly was the first to shake off her surprise.

Delores swatted Beverly's arm, "She asked if anybody might have a grudge, what does that sound like? Sounds like it's suspicious at best. I would check his regular work, dear," She dropped her voice to a conspiratorial whisper. "I always felt he was shifty, he could have a cheating husband angry over photos he took or something. It's a seedy job." Delores pursed her lips yet again.

They didn't have any more information, but I couldn't

break away until I swore I would let them help in any investigation. They had come in handy in the past.

I was almost to my townhome when I saw a car pull up in front of Mason's place and a tall blonde woman get out. She barely rang the doorbell when Mason opened the door. I must have stopped and stared because Mason saw me over the woman's shoulder and stared back. Then the blonde woman turned to look at me. *Gulp.*

I power-walked the rest of the way and didn't slow down until I had slammed my door shut. Sure, we were broke up. Sure, he saw Liam holding my hand. It still stung a bit... *okay a lot. So much for hoping.... Well, that was all over.*

I went to my little back patio with all the flowerpots and began transferring the starter flowers I had bought into the pots. I made record time and bonus; I didn't hurt any flowers in the process. I was making a compact oasis in the privacy of my back patio, which means I don't have use my front porch and worry about seeing Mason or vice versa. It helped me calm down too. If Mason had moved on with this new woman, then I had my answer about any potential patching up the relationship.

I couldn't face much to eat, so a small bowl of leftover chili over corn chips was all I could stomach. I barely managed to finish that. Calmer didn't mean over it, just a sad sort of acceptance. *Heavy sigh.* I didn't play one single song on my clarinet, no time and I was a bit deflated.

I was back at my desk by seven-thirty, feeling restless. Chad had left the security tapes at the reception desk for me. Five days worth of DVDs, was in a large boot box. I clearly hadn't thought about how many hours that really amounted to, from multiple cameras too.

I was looking though the CDs and sorting them by camera location when I heard a throat clearing. My head snapped up. Liam was leaning against my door frame dressed in a Hawaiian shirt, matching shorts, and nice leather flip-flop sandals. As much as I like a sharp-dressed man, yes I know that's a song, seeing his casual and nice legs was more distracting. He held up a take-out bag from a local fish 'n chips place.

"I didn't know England was big on Hawaiian shirts. But I guess tweed is too hot." I teased.

"I went on holiday last year and got an original. I was planning on a trip to India to see the Taj Mahal and New Delhi, but my sister decided to get married." he held out the bags. "You shared the food truck experience with me, this is the closest I could do on short notice for British food. The *hush puppies* aren't something I'm familiar with though." He smiled his more genuine smile.

"Not positive, but I believe they originate from the southern states. Not surprising you haven't heard of them." I swallowed and took in a breath. Mason had been on my mind and I had forgotten all about Liam joining me. His thoughtfulness hurt at the moment though. I had to admit I wished it were Mason working on this with me.

He sat in the visitor chair on the opposite side of my desk and opened the bag. "I took a chance you may not have eaten or would be peckish." He studied me and stopped removing Styrofoam containers from the bag. "You look sad, what's happened?"

I looked away. I hated being so transparent. How do people hide their feelings? Because I really wanted to study and get that down so I could hide whatever I was thinking.

"Nothing," I held up a handful of DVDs, "We have security recordings from the last five days to review from different cameras around the resort main grounds. We haven't gone to Cloud storage because of hacking concerns, so we're stuck with these." I figure we didn't have them stored on the network more for cost issues.

"I was going to ask if you could get those. Should I get my laptop and we can split the work?" He was still watching me like a bug under a microscope.

"That's an excellent idea." Because then he would be busy watching his own footage and not trying to figure me out.

We finished eating before he got his laptop. He was looking for an electrical outlet and the only accessible one was a multi-outlet strip on my desk next to me. He reached over and we were face to face.

I said my office was tiny, but imagine a closet with just enough space to cram a basic desk, a vertical file cabinet and two chairs with barely room to maneuver between them. Cozy is a polite description. Maybe I should have arranged for a better place for this work so we wouldn't be oh so close, alone, at night, in the quiet.

"It's the bloke who saw me holding your hand, isn't it?" I could smell his sophisticated cologne with a pinch of exotic spice.

"Yes, and there's nothing to talk about." I tried for confident, but my voice came out reserved.

He looked deep into my eyes and I wondered how well he could read me because I felt as though he was looking into my very soul. Could his training make him even better at reading people? *So not fair.* I swallowed several times.

"Okay, but I'm a good listener if you'd like to talk." He moved back to his laptop.

I had to change the subject, "Oh, I've got more on Rick Rogers competing to get on a reality show, something like Real Investigations. He and his competition, Mike Hammond, got into a fistfight the last episode."

"So maybe it was a matter of money or status and he got killed to remove the competition? It wouldn't be the first time." He busied himself with his laptop.

"Have you heard from Detective Lawrence on the official verdict?" I avoided making eye contact and focused on the security disks.

"He called and said preliminary verdict is poison, but they haven't identified what poison and it could be awhile to get results from the lab." His laptop beeped as it powered up.

Who poisoned somebody in this day and age? That was so old school. The modern age is all about fast death, a gun being the fastest. But poison was slower and took planning.

"I'm thinking we start with the oldest recordings and make our way forward." I held up a print out of Rick Rogers photo, "This is the guy we're looking for to figure out what he was doing here."

"You thinking what I'm thinking?" He raised his eyebrows.

That was such a loaded trick question.

He smiled, "That he was investigating somebody, maybe following a cheating spouse even."

We fast-forwarded through our respective DVDs trying to spot the deceased man. After about two hours, I was in the middle of my second DVD with the camera angle covering the shaded walkway around the lake. The camera was a safety measure since that section can be dark and a little spooky if you are alone.

I saw a couple walking, at one point she was up against a tree and they really needed to find a room. They finally walked on and shortly I saw a guy carrying a camera with a telephoto lens follow.

"I think I found our Mr. Rogers." I couldn't help it, that was his name.

CHAPTER 5

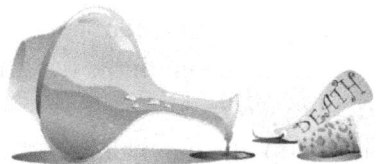

*L*iam leaned over my right shoulder as I reversed the recording up to the couple just coming into view. We watched them get very amorous against a tree, the man's hands going places that should only be done in private. I was aware of Liam's closeness and his cologne as we watched their passionate interlude. *Awkward.*

Finally the couple moved out of camera view and the private detective strolled along following the couple from a distance, his camera with a telephoto lens in one hand behind his back.

"Well bugger, I don't think we can get a decent still image of either the man or woman since that was a rather dark spot. Rather cheeky of them."

"I know I'm going to suggest we post a sign next to that tree stating there's a camera watching. Maybe that'll keep such eager couples from stopping there again." I felt my face heat up, I was no doubt blushing several shades of red.

"That was around 2:36 in the afternoon on the first day," I stuck to facts. "Let's focus around that time and forward on the other camera angles."

At midnight we had gone through all of the first three days of recordings and had several instances were Rogers was clearly surveilling the same couple.

"I can't focus anymore. I think we have enough for now." I covered a big yawn.

"We can finish up the recordings in the morning. I don't think it'll take too long since we can spot the couple easily now." Liam looked as tired as I felt. Maybe he was fighting London time still.

"I want to take the screen shots we took of the couple and see if they're staying here at the hotel. I'll ask at the restaurants and room service." I managed while fighting off another yawn.

"Room service is a good call. I'd focus on the first day when they stopped and couldn't restrain themselves as a good bet for eating in," he added. "I'd even wager that recoding was the day they checked in by how eager they were. Looked like an affair and they'd been apart for a while." He avoided my eyes.

"I wonder if he might be Mr. Marks?" That would make short work of this.

I jogged to my car in the lot, grateful I had brought a lightweight coat from home. It was a new moon and the only illumination came from the streetlights. With each breath I smelled moisture in the air. The only sounds were a distant car, a few people leaving the Gilded Hornet pub, and the yipping of a coyote from the golf course. I scrambled into my car faster than might have been necessary, relaxing when I locked all the doors.

I had just parked my car in my garage and was getting out when I saw Mason with his Sheltie, Roulette, on a leash standing on the sidewalk watching me arrive home very late on a work night. I was never this late on a work night. It was rather late to be walking his dog, even for him. I waved to him but couldn't see his expression.

If he didn't have ideas before, he sure did now. I knew he was thinking I'd been out with Liam. I slammed my hand against the button to close the garage door. I was too tired to deal with what he was thinking. *Great, just great. At this rate we'll never get back together.*

My sleep was plagued with dreams of Mason and I moving further apart, in separate cars, trains, planes, boats, even canoes going opposite directions. I woke up in a funk.

I dragged myself into work and began scanning the surveillance recordings again. I just wanted to uncover why Rick Rogers had been so interested in this resort and keep our name from any connection to another murder.

Before long I was interrupted with return calls from the musicians, floral shop, and the cake vendor regarding the upcoming nuptials that took an hour to get them directions on how to deliver goods or setting up at the venues on our property. I would have to meet with the floral shop people to show them the new wedding venue for their planning. That would be this afternoon.

"Sorry I'm late." Liam's voice sounded from my door. Today he wore slacks and a simple button down shirt.

"No tropical theme today?" I teased.

"Not during business hours if we're going to go over the rest of those recordings." He stood with one hand hidden around the door jamb.

"Are you hiding something there secret agent man? Hey do you get a number? Are you one-oh-seven?" I smiled to let him know I wasn't serious. I was keeping up appearances when I really wanted to pull the covers over my head at home.

He revealed a pressed cardboard carrier with two coffees and a pastry bag. *How was it this man wasn't married? Why was it that in spite of his drop dead gorgeous looks and thoughtful ways I was only minimally attracted or interested?*

"You didn't have to go to all this trouble, really."

"No trouble." He scrutinized me, "You look knack-ered. Did a good night's sleep elude you?"

Well, that was brutally honest. "No worries, I'm as good as new." Not really, but close enough. "Thanks for breakfast."

I was reminded just how close of quarters my office was again when he came in and settled down in the visitor chair.

The dark roast aroma filled the office and my mind woke a little from the smell alone. One cup wasn't going to last me today, but it was a start.

He turned on his laptop that had stayed on my desk overnight. While it was booting up he gave me a choco-late chip Croissant from the bag. We bumped cardboard coffee cups and settled in to watch the last of the surveillance recordings.

The coffee and croissants were long gone and it was

an hour and a half later when he finished first and waited. It took me another ten minutes.

I turned from my monitor and faced him, "okay, let's see what we've got." I motioned for him to go first.

He looked at the notes he had taken. "Okay. Day one I didn't find anything, but day two I have Rogers watching the couple eat at the hotel's lakeside patio for brunch. Rogers sat a little apart from them and I think he used his cell phone to take pictures. Day three I have them walking past in the evening dressed up like going to dinner and Rogers isn't far behind them. I couldn't tell if they were eating here or going out," he turned his notepaper over and continued. "Day four I got nothing. Day five they are strolling around the lake without any public displays of affection. The couple did stop and were talking and Rogers ducked behind a tree for a while waiting on them, then he seems to see something else and leaves. As far as I can tell he stopped tailing the couple. The morning of his death I see him alone walking around the hotel and again near the grand ballroom." He looked up and motioned for my turn.

"Day one was where I have them frisky on the lake-walk against the tree. Day two I have them entering one of the jewelry stores on property and Rogers trying to take photos from outside with his telephoto lens. Day three nothing." I cleared my throat for the next part, "Day four I have a glimpse of Rogers walking around like he's trying to find them but no sign of them anywhere. Room service that day is a good bet since neither of us saw any sign of the couple. Day 5 is strange I see Rogers occasionally but no sign of the couple and that continues on yesterday when he died. I do have where he approached me at the front entrance, but he leaves right after talking to me."

I looked up and he handed me his notes. "Don't you need a copy?"

"Nope, I memorized it plus what you told me just now." His tone was matter-of-fact, like it was no big deal.

"Uh huh, okay one-oh-seven. Well this mere mortal appreciates the notes." I put his in the same spiral note-book I had my notes.

He sat back in the guest chair and looked at me expectantly. It finally hit me he was waiting for what to do now.

Before I could say what I planned next, Chad popped his head in and seemed startled to see Liam sitting in my office.

"Are you making any progress on the man who died?" He planted his feet apart and crossed his arms. He didn't usually take such an aggressive tone or stance. Could it be for one-oh-seven's sake?

I told him what we had found so far regarding Mr. Rick Rogers and his apparent reason for being on the resort grounds.

"I don't like that our guest's privacy was being invaded. I wish we could limit access to guests only." He put his hands on his hips.

"We've discussed it before, too much of our revenue comes from the public, either spending money at our shops, dining in our restaurants, or the membership program. Plus the golf course is used continually by non-guests too."

"I know, I know. What is your next move?"

"I think we need to ask questions of the staff who likely interacted with the couple he was following. I want to find out their names at least to turn over to the police." I glanced at Liam and he nodded.

Chad left after huffing a bit more about the rock and a hard place he was in with the public access to the hotel grounds.

"I thought we should split up and make fast work of the interviews. I'll check the room service orders and see what that provides, see if I can track down the employee who delivered the meals, particularly on day four. You could charm the waitresses at the Lakeside patio where they had lunch."

"Then maybe we can tackle the jewelry store together before lunch?" His gaze was non-committal, as if he was all business. He didn't even smile to entice me. It worked.

"Sure, we can get some soup or salad and a sandwich at Café René and sit outside on the patio." I wasn't in the mode to chase a food truck or spend much at the finer restaurants on property. Besides, I wanted to keep it very casual with Liam.

"That sounds perfect. Meet back here in, say… an hour?"

"Okay. If either is late, we'll wait for the other." I added, since I wasn't sure how long running down the room service orders was going to take.

We parted and I made my way to the accounting office first. They would have the ability to isolate room service charges in a search whereas I knew the check-in desk couldn't look up information that way. I couldn't even do searches with those parameters.

Accounting was down a few halls from my office. I used my employee identification from around my neck to open the "employee access only" area.

I walked up to the desk of a middle-aged woman who wrapped her hair up in a retro beehive ordeal and had false eye-lashes that would occasionally start to detach as you talked with her. Her office was only slightly larger than mine.

"Hi Catherine." I waited as she maneuvered her mouse in short bursts and clicked furiously. Her eye-lashes seemed secure today.

She finally stopped and looked at me, a thin smile barely lifted the ends of her dark red mouth.

"What brings you into the numbers-game office today?" Her voice sounded like she chain-smoked, but there was never any evidence of even a vapor or electronic cigarette.

I told her what I needed.

"Three days ago, huh? What do you need, just a room number?" She croaked out.

"Room number and name of occupants on record would be great. If there is any way to tell who delivered the items, that would be very helpful."

She studied me like I was a problem teenager who asked for the car keys along with the keys to her liquor cabinet.

"I'll wait." I tossed in for good measure.

She pursed her dark red lips, turned, and began

clacking away on her keyboard. In five minutes, maybe seven, she had a printout for me.

"Thanks Catherine, you're a gem." I said on my way out the door. I heard a mumbled reply but couldn't tell what she said. I didn't really want to know.

The printout was basic and sorted by room numbers. I scanned through the list and on the fourth page I saw breakfast, lunch, dinner, and an evening strawberries with whipped cream and champagne from the same room. Bingo. This had to be the couple. Room 327 in the new building across the lake was listed under April Johnson.

Still, it would be best to talk with the delivery person and get a description of the occupants to make sure. There was no indication on the printout who made the deliveries, so I was guessing I would make a trip to the respective restaurants the orders originated from based on the food ordered. I was still in training and room services operations were new to me.

My first stop was the Peak Bistro, a modern take on a French bistro with continental food. Apparently room 327 had ordered dinner consisting of Lobster Ravioli and Mussels.

I was assaulted with noise upon entering the kitchen area. Orders were yelled back and forth to be heard over the chopping and whisking, food sizzling or boiling, dishes clinking, and wait staff bustling in and out with dishes. The aromas all melded together for one heady perfume. It was a stainless steel world and hot. I was directed to a small table in the corner of the kitchen where room service paperwork was maintained.

"We get the orders on the computer here, but we have

to print out the order to follow the meal through prep and delivery to the room." One of the kitchen staff stopped her chopping of vegetables to explain. She had to speak loudly over the noise of the kitchen staff yelling orders and directions to one another.

"How would I find out who delivered this meal order?" I showed my printout from accounting and pointed to the room 327 order.

She typed on the computer and clicked through a few screens. "Looks like Jake delivered that one."

"Is Jake here today? I have some questions about these guests." Maybe I should have put that a better way?

"Jake has today off, but he should be back tomorrow." She didn't seem suspicious of my questions at all.

I tracked down the breakfast and lunch orders in a different restaurant and those delivery people weren't available for one reason or another. I wasn't positive this was the couple who Rick Rogers had been following. In the back of my mind I was tempted to just go knock on room 327 and see who answered to make sure.

But then what? I didn't have any plan on how to get information from them... Or did I? I had a tickling of my brain that was an idea forming. But it would have to wait; I was late getting back for Liam.

I made it to my office only five minutes late to find Liam there on his cell phone. It seemed it might be with his *job*, so I took the opportunity to check in with Chad.

I stood in his doorway, "I have a question for you?"

"What is it? I'm neck deep in budget issues." He didn't even look up from his computer monitor.

"Concerning my *extra duties as assigned*, I need to talk to some guests. They might have been why that private detective was hanging around here. How do you feel about my saying I work with security and we think they were being followed?" It was messy and not ideal, but the only thing I could come up with.

"I don't like it." He ran a hand over his chin, "Isn't there a more subtle way you could approach them? Do I have to remind you about guest privacy? That could cause them to feel their privacy is being invaded and we can't have that."

"I'll try to think of another way." There went my idea down in flames. I went back to my office and Liam was off the phone.

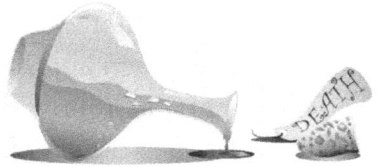

CHAPTER 6

The Colorado Springs Resort is a sprawling complex of buildings. My office is in the original hotel with its stucco façade on the east side of the lake. The complex consists of the South and West buildings, the Lakeside Suites, and the West Tower not to mention the eighteen restaurants, 185,000 square feet of meeting space, the twenty-five retail stores, golf club, tennis club, full-service spa including an indoor pool, fitness center, forty-three treatment rooms, and the hair and nail salon.

All the main facilities are situated along the circular path around the manmade lake. That doesn't include the ranch area, wilderness retreat, or the fishing camp on completely different properties from the main grounds. It was a substantial resort complex and portfolio.

Liam and I strolled over to the jewelry store in companionable silence enjoying the mild weather and several noisy birds singing an ode to spring. Any women we passed would ogle Liam, one young woman was so busy trying to catch his eye she bumped into another guest. I assumed Liam was thinking about his phone call since he was quiet and oblivious to the attention he received.

I wasn't talkative for thinking how to tactfully ask for information that might be invading a guest's privacy, which Chad had just reminded me, was sacrosanct. Not that I forgot, but there had to be a way to figure this out.

We entered the shop among a line of five stores along the entryway to the main hotel. There was a woman trying on some pearl and diamond earrings, so we had to wait for the saleslady. It was in the small shops like this peppered throughout the hotel and surrounding buildings that I was starkly reminded I couldn't afford to stay here, let alone buy the upscale merchandise. I nearly choked at the price for a baby ring.

Finally the sales lady, dressed in Channel clothes and shoes and looking as expensive as the jewelry, was free and only after her eye took in Liam and dismiss him did she turn to me. "How can I help you?"

I hadn't worked with this store in my time in training, so she likely didn't know me. "I'm the Manager in Training under Chad. I have a question for you," She nodded for me to continue. *So far, so good.* "Three days ago, did the couple in room 327 purchase anything? We know they were in here, but we're confirming the room number." It sounded incredibly lame to my ears. I just hoped she wouldn't be difficult.

She studied me intently for several long seconds, but finally glided over to her checkout stand and fingered through some manual sales receipts.

"You're in luck. Most people use a credit card not their room number. Their purchase of…" She looked at the paper again, "ruby earrings was charged to 327."

"Did they sign for it?"

She showed me the slip to charge eighteen hundred dollars to their hotel bill. I couldn't read the signature at all.

I was hesitant to ask for their names. But apparently Liam didn't have such issues.

"Their names, if I may ask?" Liam's British accent made it sound so cultured.

The saleswoman stared at me with an eyebrow raised.

"Did you hear their names at all?" I added to Liam's request.

Her cool exterior must have had a chink in it, for she abruptly shifted her gaze and crossed her arms. "I can't say. You'll have to look at the hotel registration. I believe you're very familiar with the check-in desk operations."

Ouch, that hurt. So, she knew I worked my way up from reception. *Yes, I was just common folk. Nothing wrong with that.* I lifted my chin a bit.

We left without another word. I had hoped Liam's presence would have softened her a bit, but no such luck. Rather than head for lunch, I walked directly to the reception and check-in desk with Liam not far behind. I went around to the service side and took over a computer not being used by the two ladies working the desk. They nodded to me, but otherwise left me alone. I logged in with my administration password and clicked through screens.

Whoever had been in room 327 had checked out. I

went into prior guest billing. Mr. And Mrs. Bill Smith, at least they didn't use the clichéd "Jones." They paid their bill in cash, no credit card. Dead end.

"Julienne, anything I can help with?" Cate was one of the front desk employees I had worked when I was at the front desk.

"This guest paid in cash, how would I get the name on the credit card used to hold the room?" I moved aside for her to use the keyboard. It had been awhile since I worked this position and I was rusty.

She looked at the guest record, "It's been over twenty-four hours so it's been scrubbed. The card information is retained long enough to catch any charges after checkout from room issues or items from mini-bar tallied after they vacated, but then the card is automatically removed by the system for security purposes."

I leaned closer and whispered, "I suspect they used a bogus name to cover up their tryst. Any idea how I could get their real names?"

She smiled at me, "Expensive digs for an affair." She looked over the account, "looks like you're out of luck since they had everything charged back to the room and then paid in cash. They're careful." I thanked her for helping me and arranged to have coffee with her next week to catch up.

We satat Café René and waited to share what we both found until we placed our orders. The Café had brick walls, diamond-paned windows, and red checkered table cloths, with French themed décor and pictures. I liked the bright and cheery ambience. The menu items were more French home cooking and casual than gourmet and wasn't as pricey as the other restaurants while still serving great food.

I shared my luck with room service.

"At least you got that far," Liam commented. "I didn't get so much as a room number like you. All I got was a waitress who swore both the man and woman were some-body important locally. But she couldn't put a name to them or why she vaguely recognized them."

"Our only lead and they've slipped through our fingers without much of a trace."

Our food came in quick time. They served a number of business types who needed to get back to jobs, so they were probably the fastest of the resort's dining options for lunch, along with the Gilded Hornet pub. I got my favorite gourmet chicken potpie and Liam got the onion soup with a salad.

Between savory bites I kept the conversation going, "Tomorrow I'll talk to the delivery people for the room service orders. One of them has to be working by then." I took a drink of my soda.

Café René was busy and the soft buzz of conversa-tions around us was relaxing. People were escorted to tables or leaving, wait staff bustled about taking orders and delivering meals around us. Even in the hustle and bustle Liam got winks and a few sashays from female guests.

"That's good. Maybe one of them will have recog-nized the couple, because Bill Smith is so generic it's dodgy, which is probably why they paid with quid… um cash." He took a sip of his iced tea before continuing, "If they used a credit card, their real names would likely be used and leave a trail. With cash they could use any name without having to show identification too."

"I wonder if I can find the front desk person who checked them in? It's a long shot, but one more thread to follow up on." Maybe the person who checked them in would remember the name on the card. I took another tasty bite of the flakey crust and creamy chicken filling. I wanted to moan it was so good, but that could be embarrassing. I settled for closing my eyes to savor the flavors.

"When can we take a gander at the victim's office and figure out what he was working on from there?" He had finished his salad and was half way through his onion soup.

"I have to show the florist around this afternoon for your sister's wedding and work on a few other things. Tonight I have an obligation. It'll have to be tomorrow." I noticed his raised eyebrow when I said I was busy tonight.

It was getting together with Porsche, my best friend since high school. I didn't want to reschedule again since I had rescheduled twice already. I couldn't tell if his reaction was because I wasn't working the case every spare moment of my time like last night, or if he was thinking I had a date and he was getting a little possessive.

He must have read my thoughts, or more likely saw them on my face, because he added, "I just know we have a short time to work on this." He cleared his throat, "Not that you shouldn't have a personal life. Naturally you date and don't live every moment for the job, I…" He sputtered to a stop.

I grabbed my cell phone and dialed. "Porsche, I'm working to clear the Resort from any connection on a possible murder. No, I'm not postponing again. I just need to meet later than we planned."

She sounded down, not the usual upbeat pretty blonde spitfire I knew and loved. Porsche was flexible and decided to bring food to my place so we didn't have to worry about how late we talked.

I briefly considered introducing Porsche to Liam, but that still didn't solve the time I needed to investigate on top of meet her. Liam might actually be a good distraction for Porsche, and vice versa. She was missing Vail Detective Johan Larson that we met about three and a half months ago when I assisted with his murder investigation. They had become incredibly fond of each other fast and she had been moping about since then. I might still introduce them, just not tonight.

When I say I "assisted" in the investigation, I really just gathered gossip and filtered it to the Johan who was handling weather related emergencies. The police were overwhelmed by the snowstorm from hell. I did figure out who the murderer was before everyone left the resort and could get away.

I hung up from Porsche and raised an eyebrow at Liam.

To his credit he blushed deeply, "I wasn't trying to push myself into your evening plans."

I wasn't sure if I believed that. "Sure one-oh-seven, because you aren't a smooth operator at all and you don't have women offering their phone numbers without even asking." I let a slight smile lift one side of my mouth.

After seeing the response of women around him today, I doubted he was so dedicated to his demanding job that he didn't date. I mean, look at him. He had Hollywood, or Bollywood, actor good looks and women clearly found him appealing. Just the women where he worked had to be angling for dates and I didn't believe for a moment he was celibate.

"I suppose I deserved that." He lowered his voice before saying, "It's probably best to keep my employer quiet, though." Then he winked at me.

I nodded, "Noted. But, I thought you were public relations and not a secret agent? I'll keep it quiet just in case."

We finished and paid separately for lunch. When Liam wasn't looking, I took a few photos with my phone with the intention of seeing if Porsche might show him around and let me investigate on my own. I managed two photos before hiding my phone away and departing.

I had a long to-do list to finish before I would be done for the evening. Not least of which was showing the cake baker and florist around for Ariya's wedding that was fast approaching.

Time flew by and I was working on the LPGA tournament again when I noticed it was time for the florist. I just arrived in the lobby to find Ariya herself standing with a man wearing a polo shirt with the florist shop name embroidered on his left side.

"Ariya, I didn't realize you'd be joining us. Did I miss something?" Did I forget an appointment or to do something for the bride-to-be?

"No, I was going through my checklist with the wedding vendors and thought I would join in today... if that's not intruding too much." She said it pleasantly, but

I got the impression that she expected me to accommodate even if it was an imposition. I respected that she wasn't being pushy, but she wasn't a push-over either. Besides, with the last minute nature of the location change for the wedding, we all needed to double-check everything.

I led the way to the ballroom, showing the florist where to park and the door to use for entry in a few days. The florist taking measurements and drawing a layout of the wedding space leaving Ariya and I to ourselves.

"My father-in-law was surprised that you were looking into that man who died in his car." Her pleasant voice with a slight British accent broke through my thoughts. At my apparent surprise she added, "Liam mentioned he was forgoing last evening with the family to help you."

"I should've realized he was missing time with you to assist. I'm sorry about that." Could I just be an excuse to avoid a stuffy family time with in-laws? I sat down in one of the few chairs left in the open room.

She laid a hand on my arm, "Oh, don't worry about that. I'm happy he is so captivated with your company." She smiled brightly, but I wanted to drop off the ends of the earth.

"Ummm, it's not like that. He's lending his expertise." I was getting flustered.

"Let me assure you, he's a gentleman and will respect your wishes, but I believe he'll prove... attentive, should you wish to spent more time with him." She looked directly in my eyes and showed no awkwardness in the least.

I, on the other hand, began choking and the florist

came running and pounded on my back until the coughing fit passed. My eyes were all watery, lashes wet, and a blush burning my cheeks.

The florist went back to his drawing, glancing my way across the room with curiosity. I was mortified.

"I'm sorry to have shocked you so. I wish him to find happiness like I have. He needs a woman who will challenge him besides just capture his eye. You are well matched." I felt like she was sizing me up as a sister-in-law too. The heat from my cheeks had become a full-blown hot flash from embarrassment.

When did sisters become matchmakers? Not having any siblings, rather two cousins instead, I couldn't be sure. But my whole family, from my father to my aunt and uncle, even my cousin Felicia were trying to marry me off, which I had put my foot down and ended. Now I had clients trying to marry me off.

"Thank you for the kind words, but I'm…" I gripped the sides of the chair. How to say this without hurting any feelings? "I, um, I just recently broke up with my boyfriend and I'm not ready to see anybody. Really, I'm not."

"Well, let's change the subject. Have you had much luck with this man's death that Liam's assisting you in?"

I took a moment to switch gears and answer. "We're just finding out who the man was and if he had any business here at the resort. That's all." Okay, maybe that was the limit of what Chad wanted, but I had a growing feeling the resort was somehow involved, even if not directly, and I might have to dig deeper than scratching the surface.

The florist discussed where the archway would be placed with Ariya, the flowers he ordered and how they could position them in the new venue and then noted everything on his diagram.

Between the matchmaking and questions about the deceased private investigator, I was delighted when the florist was done and I could part company with Ariya. Before she left, she reminded me to check on the personal cake for her diabetic mother-in-law for the reception.

The time finally approached when I was done for the day and Liam appeared at my office door. Right on time to get some snooping done.

"How should we approach this?" Liam's smooth voice was like a caress and my mind wandered to Ariya's comment. I had no doubt he would be attentive. I banished such thoughts all together; no good would come of letting my mind wander to his merits when my heart ached for somebody else.

"I've been thinking about that. My objective is to get access to his cases somehow. We should have a cover story for why we're interested in Rogers' files, but I haven't come up with what the cover could be." *That's right, focus on the dead guy and not on the slight attraction you're feeling. It's natural with a handsome virile guy like Liam, just keep a firm grasp on your thoughts.*

"What if we say we're from the network of the reality show?" His eyes sparkled.

"Why would the network be interested in Rogers' files?" I liked the idea, but it had to make sense.

Liam ran a hand across his late afternoon stubble and my mind began to wander. In the close quarters of my office his sheer masculine presence and enticing cologne captured my thoughts. I mentally slapped myself and looked away.

"Well, maybe we can say he was supposed to get some signed forms to us and hadn't sent them yet. Or, maybe we needed notes from the cases that aired." His voice exuded excitement as if this were more play than serious. Considering who he worked for, it might be more like entertainment.

"I don't know how television contracts work, but hopefully others in the office won't either. I say we go with both of those to cover our bases." I was grateful my mind was still firing at all with how distracted I was getting. I only hoped we got access to the files or I might be tempted to break in.

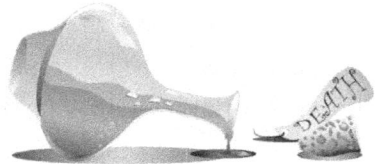

CHAPTER 7

We arrived at the office of Roderick (Rick) Rogers located in a forgotten section a few blocks from downtown. The older squat red brick strip mall contained six offices, each with a large picture window for their business name on the glass. Parking was on the side of the building with the blacktop cracked and weeds growing in the crevices. A popular bar sat on the corner that had been in business for decades.

Liam and I stood at the closed door and darted a final look at each other. We both nodded our heads. We were as ready as we could be. We had gone over our cover story again on the drive over, so this was it.

He opened the door and let me enter first, his hand on my lower back. Yesterday his touch didn't do anything for me, but today I found contact disconcerting. *Focus. Remember, it's only natural, nothing more.*

The office was even smaller than I expected from the outside. The flickering fluorescent lighting revealed a narrow oblong space with walls painted light gray and not one picture. It smelled of dust, stale air, and old carpet.

Directly inside the door a middle-aged woman with silver highlights in her long straight hair sat at a gray metal desk. A nameplate identified her as Peggy Faire, secretary. Behind her desk several feet back was an office with the door closed, no doubt that was Mr. Rogers' office. Ms. Faire's gray eyes regarded us.

Liam jumped in while I was still getting my bearings. "Hello, we're with the reality show, Real Investigators. I'm Bryce and this is Angela." He was good at ad-libbing, because we hadn't discussed names at all. I could have been stuck with Fern or Betty. "We just visited Mr. Hammond and need to finish a few things up with Mr. Rogers."

She cringed; either at the use of "Mr. Rogers" or that she might have to inform us of his demise.

I hurried to smooth the way, "don't worry, we know he's deceased. We simply have to pick up some documents he was planning on providing during our visit." I flashed a smile but worried it was more a scowl.

"Your visit isn't on the calendar and he didn't say anything to me." Once she spoke her pain became evident, her voice was lackluster as if sadness weighted her vocal chords.

Liam jumped in, if anything could get her heart pumping his low sultry voice would do the trick, "We spoke to him just a few days ago about our visit, he mayn't have had an opportunity to inform you before... you know." He bent over to look her directly in the eyes,

"I hate to put you in such a position, but we're on a tight schedule to finish up and catch a plane."

He sure knew how to spin a tale which gave me pause. Maybe I shouldn't trust everything he said either. Or, maybe that was my own issues bubbling up into the situation. Still, made me think.

"I can get them, what sort of papers were they?" She offered.

I jumped at the idea of her pulling files for us, "A copy of the signed contract with the studio and files from his last three months of cases for us to review in the final determination. Which, we'll still go through with, even if he wins postmortem." I held my breath. Would the request give us away?

She stood up slowly, like a sloth and unlocked the office door behind her. I heard a few drawers open, but I also heard a hushed voice. I glanced at Liam and he held his finger up to his lips to indicate not to say anything.

Liam walked to the open office door with me right behind him. Peggy Fair was on a cell phone talking, her back to us.

"Nobody from the studio came by your place needing files from the last three months? Then who are these two...?" She turned and spotted us watching her. She gulped. "Look Hammond, in case I'm found dead here's a photo."

She lifted the cell phone to take a photo, and we ducked to the side of the door. This wasn't going according to plan, but then why should this be any different from all our attempts so far?

"I can explain Ms. Faire. But we need to talk calmly."

I was hoping to still salvage something from our visit. "We're looking into his death and just trying to figure out if anything he was working on... you know."

"Why should I believe you when you've already lied to me? Tell me that, huh? I'm not stupid you know." She had some fire now. So glad I could be of assistance with that.

"Well, he had my name on him and the police already questioned me. I didn't know him and wanted to figure out why he had my name. My friend is with me to try to keep me out of trouble." The words just tumbled out, but I guess that was really why I was going to such trouble.

I glanced at Liam and shrugged my shoulders.

He leaned into me and whispered, "I don't want to stay in the good ole mate zone, you know that don't you?" And then gave me a slow kiss on the cheek. I was enveloped by the scent of his soap and aftershave.

Focus Julienne, for goodness' sake, focus! It was a little peck on the cheek, no big deal.

When I looked away from Liam's milk chocolate eyes, I found Peggy standing in the door watching us. I couldn't speak and my face was on fire.

"Now that kiss was real. I believe you aren't here to necessarily hurt me. I still don't know if I can trust you seeing as how Rick's passing is a suspicious death and all."

Liam turned his hungry eyes to Peggy and in a husky voice suggested we sit and talk. Peggy gulped and looked at me.

"I don't know how you're resisting honey, 'cause he's turning my legs to Jello just talking."

In my mind's eye I saw Mason when we first met and

he kissed my hand. I resisted Liam because I still hoped for my Mason to realize the error of his ways so we could be a couple again. But, the longer things went unresolved with Mason, the more I wondered why I wasn't moving on.

"Let's just sit and talk, please." I motioned to the few chairs that made up the tiny waiting area against the large shop window in front of Peggy's desk. On the inside the sun struggled to penetrate the grimy windows.

Peggy led the way. We barely got seated when she started, "So, are you really the person whose business card was found on him?"

I explained who I was, and that I worked at the resort. "He asked me about a Mr. Marks. I didn't give him a card nor did I give him any information since I'm not allowed to. So the police came to ask about it and my manager wants to clear the Resort of any involvement."

"Are you the woman who figured out who killed the Pastor last fall? Rick… I mean Mr. Rogers was surprised an amateur could figure it out on her own." She was looking at me with appraising eyes now. "I'm thinking you might do okay looking into his death. I never knew him to be impressed by another's work, but he was with you."

Was she going to give me the files? "So, you're saying…?"

"I'll make copies, but you'll have to sign a confidentiality agreement. That's a must." She stood up and waited for my response.

"Yes, absolutely. That's not a problem, because turning anything over to the police didn't count. I'll lock them up too." I was surprised by her words. A man I barely spoke to for thirty seconds had thought well of me. The reality was sad. Could that have something to do with why he spoke to me, why he asked me about Mr. Marks? How was this all intertwined?

"Can I just look around his office, in case something strikes me?"

She was halfway to the back office. She stopped as if considering it, then waved for us to join her.

Liam and I trailed after her into the compact square room with a horizontal gray metal file cabinet against a side wall with books lined up on top. The title of one was "Reward: Anthology of Unsolved Crimes of the Last Three Decades."

I took my phone out and snapped some quick, quiet photos of the books and items on his desk. I looked closer at a framed photo on his desk of a dog and cat. So, Mr. Rogers was single, or a loner.

"Okay, here are the last three months or so of cases, they weren't much. But they kept the office open." She seemed sad again, her voice was flat, monotone.

Liam saw an opening and dived in, "What will happen with the office now? Will you get another PI? Join Mr. Hammond?"

She didn't appear to find the question offensive.

"I doubt it; Hammond has little overhead because his wife helps him in the office. But, I guess I'm the owner of the business now since Rick and I were partners after the last loan I floated him. I could hire another."

Her gaze fixed on me again. "Oh no, don't look at me like I'm the next Sam Spade. Never going to happen. I'm in Resort management and plan on working around the world."

Liam got a contemplative look on his face and I wondered what that was about.

Once I signed a two-page confidentiality agreement and promised to return the files when I was done with them without making personal copies, we left with what we came for. *Mission accomplished.*

It was just after the rush hour so I got Liam back to the resort in a speedy fifteen minutes. He was quiet, which made me nervous. I was silent in hopes of not discussing his kiss. Even though it was on the cheek and mild, it lingered on my mind. That wasn't how I intended things to go. He's a guest, leaving in a few days, and not who I really want.

I pulled up to let him out, I wanted to take the files home and look over them before I called it a night. Besides, I wanted to get home for my girl's night with Porsche.

He hesitated in opening his door, "I'm not sorry for the kiss, only that it wasn't on the lips. I don't know what's going on in your life. But, if you want travel like you said back there, I could help you get a job in Resort Management in London. Think about it." He stepped out of the car and trotted up the steps to the lobby.

He couldn't be serious, could he? An offer for a London Resort, be still my heart. Then there was the unspoken promise of dating a guy who was ready to be a one-woman man from the hints he dropped. That was a potent carrot he just dangled in front of me. My life-complication meter just pegged.

I was daydreaming about London Resorts like the Ritz, Savoy, Claridge's, Corinthia, the Mandarin Oriental Hyde Park, and the Dorchester. It was like dangling dice before a gambling addict. The thought of gambling brought me back to Mason again.

He played in high stakes poker tournaments and won his share. Another facet that led to his nickname Bond Jr. Oh, what was I going to do about Mason? How could I consider such an amazing offer if Mason was still on my mind and the hope we could somehow work out our big glaring problem?

I lived in a townhome my father gave me when he retired to Florida. It was a two story stucco building with red tile roof. I called it charming, my father called it old world charm.

Porsche had arrived before me and had used her key to get dinner setup for us. She is a self assured blonde with intelligence and a big heart. She used to date often and never seriously until our last adventure snowed in with a killer. She developed a fondness for the detective leading the investigation and she hasn't dated since even though he is still in Vail and she is back in Colorado Springs.

The site of Porsche with our restaurant orders already transferred from Styrofoam to plates and waiting filled me with joy. Whenever I did take a resort job away from home, I would miss my best friend terribly.

"Hey lady, I'm so glad our favorite restaurant does take out orders." She smiled bright, "Want to open the wine for us? I got the French red blend we like." She carried our meals to the living room.

I poured the wine and joined her.

Oh, this was a great way to end the day. We sat on my overstuffed navy-blue sofa with some smooth jazz music on the stereo. I took out my phone and brought up the photo of Liam I had secretly taken earlier.

I handed her the image of Liam looking stone-cold fine, "He's in town for a few days and I thought you might like to show him around." Then I dug into my food as I curled my legs under me.

She let out a low whistle and then purred like a cat. "The perks to your job are so not fair. Typically, I would gladly entertain Mr. Temptation-walking. But…" She shrugged a shoulder and took a bite of her food.

"Still pining away for Johan?"

"I wouldn't say pining so much as… Well, we've been talking, and he's coming to visit in a few days." She took a gulp of wine, "Am I crazy to hold out hope for a long distance relationship to work?" She looked directly into my eyes.

What to say? I liked Johan, respected him tremendously and thought he was good for Porsche. But, he was a homicide detective, which was dangerous. Maybe it wasn't as dangerous as narcotics or a beat cop, but still dangerous. He could get hurt, or worse, and Porsche was already over-the-moon for him.

Then again, who was I to talk? I had broken up with Mason and was holding out hope it would work out in spite of all the signs it wouldn't.

"The heart wants what it wants and you are the only one who can answer that for yourself." Not the advice she wanted, but it was the best I could do.

"Did you just string together two trite answers for me?" She whacked my shoulder with a decorative throw pillow.

She took a bite of her steak and looked at the photo of Liam again. She swallowed, "My goodness girl, you sure attract the gorgeous guys. What's his story?"

"British and Indian here for his sister's wedding I'm coordinating." It was an abbreviated version, but I had more important things to discuss. "Did you hear about the guy who died in his car and caused an accident?"

"I heard something, but I don't know details. What about him?" She answered before another bite of steak.

Between bites of my pasta with pesto and salmon I explained who Roderick Rogers had been and how Chad wanted me to investigate. I covered everything, but excluded Liam helping me. For some reason I was happy to pawn him off on her, but didn't want to admit he was helping me investigate. Was I feeling guilty for feeling attracted to Liam in spite of the fact Mason and I weren't a couple?

"Back to the original topic, why are you trying to hand this Liam from England over to me? I can tell when you're holding back all the details, you know?" She pointed her fork at me in emphasis.

"I uh, he's uh, well I just…" I filled my mouth with pasta and chewed slowly.

"You're too easy to read. Let me guess. He's flirted, and you experienced a bit of attraction but you're pining for Mason. Ergo you feel guilty or something." She chuckled softly.

I almost choked on my pasta, "Can we change the subject please?" I took a gulp of wine.

She nodded. "So, tomorrow you may find out the identity of the couple dead PI guy was following and you have the files to go through. Sounds like you'll be able to clear the resort pretty fast at this rate." She stopped eating and studied me, a frown developing.

"Out with it. There's something bothering you and I don't think it's some stranger's murder." She continued to stare at me.

I really had to learn to how to keep my feelings from showing.

"Mason saw me with that Liam fellow at the resort and acted like, well like it was more than it was. Then yesterday a leggy blonde was at his door."

She sat down her dish with a few bites left of her meal, "Honey, I love you. But you don't have a clue about guys."

I let out a frustrated sigh, I may have even rolled my eyes.

"So, this Liam guy, is he interested in you? Men sense when another guy is looking at the woman they want. I think it's a Neanderthal thing that they haven't evolved past." She smiled to show she wasn't entirely serious about the Neanderthal remark.

I started to say no, Liam wasn't interested in me seriously. But the offer he made to help get me a resort job in London and the clear message with that to see him romantically slapped me cold in the face. Then there was the kiss on the cheek and his flat out telling me he wanted more than friendship.

I attempted to reply a few times and stopped, only to try again and stop. I must've looked like a fish struggling for air.

"Uh, huh. He's interested in you. Maybe even more than a little." I know she thought she was going easy on me, but it didn't feel that way on my end. It felt like my dad interrogating me after a date.

"But he barely knows me, and he's leaving in a few days." She didn't need to know his proposal.

How had I gotten into this mess with Liam and Mason? I didn't intend to encourage one or shut down the other. *Oh crap, crap, crap. Did I mention I'm terrible with men?*

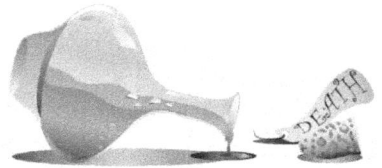

CHAPTER 8

*P*orsche and I talked for hours over the rest of dinner, dessert, and more wine. I didn't get to Rogers' files before collapsing in bed.

I had weird dreams of being on the retro dating game show with Mason and Liam being contestants. The show ended with the two of them fighting and my leaving. Another dream was about glasses of wine being poisoned and my trying to figure out which one before I drank some.

So, my morning was rough, and I wasn't in the mood for Liam today and the day after tomorrow was his sister's wedding rehearsal and dinner.

I finished a tense phone call with a major sponsor for the LPGA golf tournament who wanted their custom vinyl banner displayed in the hotel. Tacky advertising hanging between fluted marble columns wasn't going to happen. A distinct clearing of a throat drew my attention to my neighbor Delores standing in my doorway holding a bag.

Other than Mason, there were few of my neighbors that frequented the resort and fewer that visited me. I smiled and felt special.

"I won't take much of your time, dear. But, I wanted to get these to you right away." She handed me the plain paper bag.

Inside I found DVDs of the "Real Investigators: Season 2" with a note specifying which shows had Rogers or his competitor Hammond, or both in an episode.

"I had no idea you were such a huge fan that you owned the series."

"Oh, I ran out and bought those for you. I went through them to make the notes. I figured this would help your investigation." I was gobsmacked.

I went over and gave her a huge bear hug. "That was very thoughtful. Thank you so much, I'll reimburse you."

She waved my offer aside.

"Am I interrupting something?" The spiced chocolate voice with a sprinkling of English accented intruded.

Liam had just joined us and was showing his mischievous smile. I thought Delores was going to exhaust herself from batting her eyes at him until she opted to pat her hair. Delores usually went for the Firefighter type, as in the Firefighter calendar pin up types, but she seemed to warm to Liam's slim but athletic build and his smooth charm.

I dropped the bag into the guest chair, "No, this is my neighbor Delores. She stopped by catch me up on gossip. This is Liam, a guest at the hotel."

I let them chat, or rather Liam made small talk while sixty-something Delores flirted shamelessly.

Finally, she turned to me, "I have to get some errands done." She winked and mouthed *ooh la la* to me.

News of Liam would be all over the Mountain Shadows townhomes. *Great, just great.* I hoped Mason didn't hear any of it.

Delores had left and was well out of hearing range before I turned to Liam, "I'm swamped here with work, so it's best if we reconvene tomorrow."

He studied me for a full minute, his gaze searching my face. "I understand, yesterday was a lot to take in. You need to think. We can resume the case tomorrow." He smiled and slowly turned to leave.

I breathed a sigh of relief. I liked him, and there was a growing attraction. But, it really was too fast, and I didn't know how to take the offer of resort employment in London. It was a lot, and I definitely needed time to think. Besides, I was tired of the intrusion into my limited workspace.

I shut the office door and began going through the DVDs of Real Investigators that Delores had bought. Her notes allowed me to zoom to only the Rogers or Hammond parts. Over the next two hours and a half I watched the two compete in the reality show.

The individual investigations weren't that different, but their personal tactics were nothing alike. Rogers went for the flamboyant and do anything to get what he wanted approach. His competition, Mike Hammond, played to the camera, but seemed he wouldn't cross certain ethical lines. Or at least he seemed more ethical. In one case Hammond waited to search a trash can until it was outside the homes legal boundaries and on the street, whereas Rogers physically moved the trash can to the street saying, "It's my word against theirs."

The fistfight was nasty, and they clearly didn't like each other from the swearing and slinging insults. I really needed to talk to this Hammond guy.

But, now was a good time to check for the delivery people of the room service and find out the identity of the couple that Rogers had been tailing.

I locked up my office and went to the restaurants I visited yesterday. Outside a restaurant I eventually found Jake, the delivery guy for two of the meals for the couple, returning from delivery run. He was late teens and beanpole tall, which probably gave him an edge in delivery speed, and wearing the standard uniform of black pants and white shirt. We moved away from the restaurant entrance so we couldn't be overheard as people filed in and out.

I introduced myself and jumped right in, "I'm hoping you can help me with the identity of the couple you delivered these meals to a few days ago." I handed him the room service request printouts.

He scrunched his eyebrows together and looked at me.

"I understand we may have had guests of some importance and I don't think we gave them special recognition. I need to try to keep that from occurring again. You would be helping us refine our processes." *Wow, where did that come from?* It just flowed from my mouth without a thought.

He shrugged, "I don't think they wanted anybody to recognize them, so I wouldn't feel bad." His voice seemed mismatched, a masculine timber on a scrawny boy.

"I don't understand what you mean." I was playing dumb since Liam and I already suspected the couple was having an affair.

"Well… I know who they are because I've attended County Commissioner meetings and follow the local news for my political science class at the university." He looked around, making up his mind.

He looked at me again and I tried to look professional and the soul of discretion. He must have bought it, "It was County Sheriff Leland Morrison and County Commissioner Shannon Gage." He lowered his voice, "They're married – not to each other."

I know my eyes must have been nearly bulging out of their sockets and my mouth was hanging open. *Real professional LaMere.* I shut my mouth and cleared my throat.

"Are you positive? You couldn't be mistaken?" I had to ask since nobody else seemed to recognize them… except maybe the jewelry store lady.

Colorado Springs residents tend to take politics more seriously than contentious soccer matches in England. But, we had numerous workers here from other countries and they probably wouldn't recognize local political figures. I didn't because I don't follow the minutia of political happenings, but I seem to be the exception.

"I'm very sure since I've done papers on local politics and researched both of them."

I thanked him and assured him that I would keep it quiet. Which I would, the police would be the ones to deal with things ultimately if it came to that.

But, this only explained why Rick Rogers was hanging around the resort stalking them. I had to assume that somebody hired him to follow Sheriff Morrison or Commissioner Gage. That might be a spouse or political opponent, possibly somebody wants to get even with a lawman, like a person he arrested.

It didn't explain why Rogers had my name on his body when he died though. That particularly worried me. Was I involved in some way without even knowing?

I rushed back to my office. I was tempted to work on the case, but forced myself to get work for my job done since I'd spent the morning on Rick Rogers. After a few hours of my day job that included going over the upcoming wedding details and several calls to keep everyone on track, I decided to go home for lunch.

I had mixed feelings about ditching Liam, so I walked to the patio dinning and spotted him on his cell phone sitting with another man, probably his father here for the wedding. I did a covert walk by, but he was talking in hushed tones, evidently a serious conversation. So, I left with a clear conscious he was in the middle of something plus he had his father to spend time with.

Even though the weather was warming up, springtime in the Rocky Mountains was tricky and volatile with hail storms or surprise snow storms. So, I had been driving to work. I made it home in a few quick minutes. I parked in front of my townhome rather than bother with the garage. I was exiting my car when I saw the blonde woman from the other day drive up to Mason's and park in his driveway.

She got out of her car and I turned to run up the

walk and escape into my house. I had moments where I could be a chicken. I shut my door before she made it to Mason's door. She was becoming a regular. *I sighed, I'd been replaced.*

I made a salad and sandwich in record time. My main objective in running home was for more information from my neighbors. I jogged to the mailboxes and waited a few moments. It didn't take long before Delores and Nathan joined me.

Nathan was a retired Doctor with his white hair in a ponytail who is our one-man neighborhood watch. He had connections that were often useful.

Nathan started talking the instant I was in hearing range, "I hear tell you're looking into that Private Di…" Delores elbowed him in the rib cage and cut him short.

"I told him, hope you don't mind. Did those tapes help you dear?" She was even more birdlike in her mannerisms with her long neck and head cocked to the side.

I didn't bother to explain the difference between tapes and DVDs since it probably wouldn't stick, anyway.

"Guys, I need as much information as I can get on Rogers. By chance do you know anybody, the friend of a friend who knew him maybe?" I wasn't too proud to ask my backup team for help. They had assisted last fall and proved they could dig up the gossip.

Nathan smiled his tobacco stained grin, "I can put out some feelers alright. Somebody we know must have the dirt on the guy. Are you thinking he was doing something illegal and got himself killed?" Nathan was raring to go, perhaps a bit too much. I bet he read spy novels too.

"Whoa, let's not get ahead of ourselves. We don't really know much of anything. There's no indication so far about anything illegal, sheesh." I gave him a playful punch in the arm and he rocked like I really socked him.

"Do you recognize these two people?" I showed them a printout of a freeze frame from the security video of the restaurant that showed both the alleged Sheriff and Commissioner's faces. The photo was poor quality, but the best I had.

"It's pretty fuzzy there. You know who they could be? They look like Sheriff what's his name... oh drat... you know who I mean." Nathan's memory for names was wearing out lately.

Delores was examining the printout. "I guess. Sure it could be the Sheriff, but the gal really resembles that County Commissioner. I attend the city council meetings, not the County meetings so much anymore. But I think she looks like..." She thought for a bit and snapped her fingers, "Gage, don't remember the first name. Yep, looks like her." She looked at me and cocked her head like a robin.

That was pretty good confirmation to me. I brought the photo because I didn't want to follow up on them as suspects without more certainty of their identity. I didn't want a photo from online just in case they weren't who the delivery boy thought. But Delores and Nathan pretty much confirmed it.

"They involved with this? Cause there's plenty of gossip about them. He let power go to his head, even feuding with other county agencies." Nathan crossed his arms.

"I hear that Gage woman only seems to vote in ways that benefit her or her family. Crooked as can be." She shook her head and pursed her lips.

"Well, ask your connections about them and Rogers. I hate to say it, but I need the gossip, the behind-scenes-scoop. Can you help me?"

"Sure thing, we got this." He winked.

Delores swatted him, "You're a mischievous old coot."

"You're a pushy old bitty." He shot back at her.

Nice to know some things never changed.

After Nathan asked why I didn't make the pinochle group in the clubhouse last week, we parted.

I strolled back to my car, completely forgetting I wanted to avoid seeing or being seen by Mason's lady visitor.

The blonde woman was standing at his front window and came running over before I could get into my car.

"Hello, can I talk with you? It'll only take a moment." Blondie had a surprising voice, like she had competed in debate or speech: clear and authoritative without being abrasive.

"I really must get back to work." I reached for my car door handle.

"He's not here, he'll never know we talked." She looked me directly in the eyes, no flinching and shrinking. She was tall for a woman, maybe five eight, she wore designer jeans and a sophisticated blouse with a gold choker necklace and button earrings. Her blonde hair was cut in a style that softened her strong jaw and her greenish eyes had some fire.

"I don't know what to say. I hope you're happy together?" Wow, that sounded really bad even to my ears.

"What? Oh, no. You've got the wrong idea." She held out her hand, "I'm Marisa. Mason's sister." She smiled just a little. She did have Mason's jaw and eye color.

"Oh! I feel so foolish." That was all I could think to reply because I had no idea what to say to her other than the obvious "m" themed names.

"Can we chat for a little bit? I'd like to understand more about what went wrong between you and Mason."

"I can make it very simple. He promised he wasn't a playboy or Don Juan, that he wanted to be serious in a relationship." I closed my eyes and took a deep breath before continuing, "Our first months we had very little time together, which I understood until he took the body-guard job for a Hollywood starlet. The job isn't the issue. The issue is his posing as her boyfriend for the entire world to see."

I opened my eyes to see Marisa standing before me, her eyebrows raised and her mouth in a big "Oh."

"That's not the worst of it. When we sat down to talk about it, he actually said I was overreacting." I was pleased to see her expression of deepening surprise. "So I told him to look me up when he was ready to be serious and adjust his life to include a relationship."

I crossed my arms feeling a little defensive. This was his sister and no doubt she would want to defend him.

"Thank you for telling me your side of what happened. He's upset and miserable, but naturally he didn't mention any of that." She leaned against my car, making it impossible for me to leave unless I wanted to be downright anti-social.

"I like you and from just this little talk, you're good for him. His mother excused his acting out because our dad was… is so hard on him. Women have given into him far too easily. But you don't let him get away with his single-guy mindset."

I wasn't expecting praise from Mason's sister and it took me by surprise. She was a bit too direct for just meeting her and I was incredibly uncomfortable. My face was warm and I couldn't meet her eyes.

"I… um, I should really get back to…" I was blowing my strong woman image already.

"Oh, I'm sorry. I don't want to make you late." She shoved off from my car, "I'm going to work on him. Try to get him to understand your point of view. No promises."

Then, she further surprised me by wrapping me in a bear hug and clapping me soundly on the back.

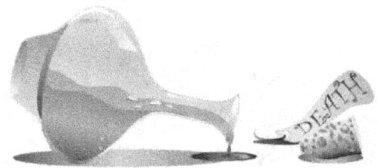

CHAPTER 9

I rushed back to work in a daze. I just met Mason's sister, behind his back, and she was going to "work" on him. Did that mean some sensitivity training? Would he be mad if he found out we were talking?

Thinking about how Marisa knew little of what happened made me wonder just what Mason had taken away from our breakup. I sat up taller in my office chair. I was waiting around hoping he would wake up and make amends. Well, that had been a waste of time, apparently. How much hope should I place in Marisa getting through to him?

Chad interrupted my annoyance with Mason, "How are your extra duties *as assigned* coming along?" He didn't look happy.

"Some progress, but I'm still not sure why my name was on his... um with him when he died." I hedged, not knowing how much he really wanted of the details.

"What does 'some progress' mean?" He ran a hand

through his blond hair making it look like he had stuck his finger in a light socket. "Look, I've managed to foster a friend at the paper and he has warned me tomorrow's edition will mention the business card on the dead man and our brush with murder last fall." His look turned more serious.

"I'll explain, but shut the door. This is sensitive information." I proceeded to share what I knew so far about the room service kid swearing he recognized the County Sheriff and Commissioner sharing the room and the deceased had been following them for several days around the resort grounds.

"This information doesn't help, if anything it could get us in a lawsuit." He jumped up from the chair and paced my tiny office – three steps, whirl about, and repeat.

"I'm working on other aspects as well. I've convinced Rogers' secretary to let me look over his most recent files and I understand he was in a fierce rivalry with another local private investigator." I gauged his reaction to this information. He began chewing his thumbnail as he paced. Okay, multi-tasking. "I'm planning on talking with the other guy and going through Rogers' files."

"Look, I've a feeling we've got to get in front of this and keep the resort from more hits to its reputation. People don't want to pay five-star prices and risk ending up in the paper or even remotely close to scandal." He stopped pacing and leaned over my desk only inches from my face.

"You've got to get some scraps of meat to throw the police. They're trying to figure out how the poison was delivered let alone what poison was used." He got even closer making me squirm, "Don't tell anybody about the Sheriff and Commissioner. That could sink us." He stopped for a moment and squinted at me, "Wasn't that British fella supposed to help you"

"Yes, he gave me a hand going through the security recordings and visiting Rogers' office. He's been busy today." I wasn't sure if that would be good or bad news to Chad, who was still in my face. Literally. Since he was so close, I saw a few grey hairs I never noticed before.

"Does he know about the Sheriff and Commissioner?"

"I just found out this morning myself, so no. I haven't told him." I held my breath.

"Good. Don't tell him. I'm going to begin preparing our statement for the press and get that to them to hope-fully be included in the paper tomorrow." He opened the office door.

"I can help with that." I stood up to follow him into his office.

"No. Work on your *special* assignment as much as you possibly can. That's crucial."

He spun on his heals and I heard him muttering *damage control* before his office door slammed.

I plopped down into my chair. When it rains, it pours. What stuck out in my mind was the mention of an article that included last fall's events.

I closed my eyes and sent out a plea to the universe, *please don't let Tiffany try to hang me in the paper again.* I went to high school with Tiffany and she apparently had nurtured a nasty grudge against me over a guy standing her up for a date with me. Said guy next stood me up, so why take it out on me? Last fall I came too close to loosing my job because she tried to hang me in the paper. I was worried she might try it again.

Wasn't this a peach of a day? It just kept getting better and better.

I had actual work to do, but I guess I was to put it off for a little while.

I looked up the phone number of Mike Hammond's office and used my cell phone without a clue how I was going to proceed.

"Hammond Investigations, we dig deeper. How may I assist you today?" I was guessing this was Hammond's wife from what Peggy had said yesterday.

"Hello Mrs. Hammond, I'm with the studio about Real Investigators Show. I need to talk with Mr. Hammond. Is he available if I stop by?" I couldn't think of anything else to say, my mind went blank when she answered. I crossed my fingers she didn't know about my same story with Peggy at Rogers' office.

"I, uh… I don't know about that…"

"It really is important I talk to him right away, I'll be flying out in the morning. I need to discuss changes to the show since Mr. Rogers has passed away… and what that means for him in the competition."

"Well, I don't know. He isn't in the office."

"I can meet him anywhere. If he's busy on a case, I'll be careful to not get in his way." I had my fingers and toes crossed.

"Well, I suppose it would be alright."

I was flabbergasted it actually worked. I closed my

mouth and took down the address where I could find Mr. Hammond.

"Look for his dark red 1970 Buick Riviera. Oh, I've got another call, gotta go." She hung up.

Why should I look for his car? That just seemed odd to me.

I considered a backup to go talk to Hammond about his rivalry with Rogers.

Porsche was in the middle of classes and I probably wouldn't see her for a few days. I grabbed my cell phone and called my cousin Felicia. Felicia was a couple years my junior, more voluptuous, and was a good sidekick when she wasn't trying to dress me in trendy and girly clothes.

It was a short conversation; she was working at her stylish consignment clothing store until closing tonight. I didn't want to turn to Liam, things had moved too fast in a short time with him and I didn't trust that.

I wasn't that close to my other cousin Loring ever since I broke up with his best friend. I don't think he has forgiven me yet. That left my Aunt Regina and Uncle Lars. Yeah, that wasn't going to happen. My father charged them with my welfare when he retired to Florida and they both thought I needed to have a mundane and quiet life. They would never back me up on this.

That left me with the resort irregulars. But, I didn't have the time to go home and round up one of my neighbors to join me and I suspected they might end up more trouble, even disastrous, than helpful. I guess I was going it alone, something I didn't like to do in such a situation.

I left a note on my desk with the time and where I was

going to meet Rogers' rival detective. In the event of something going drastically wrong, at least there would be a finger pointing to where I went. I closed my door and stuck a post-it note to it saying I would be back in an hour.

I grew up in Colorado Springs and the city has grown since my childhood. When I was learning to drive, it was five or ten minutes to almost any destination. Now it was more like twenty to thirty minutes depending on the route.

The town had expanded more to the east lately, and I hated all the cookie-cutter housing developments even though they were slick and new. I mostly didn't like the focus being concentrated out east on land that used to be a dairy farm as though the rest of the city was unimportant and inconsequential.

But out east is exactly where the address to meet Hammond took me. I ended up at a recently opened restaurant. I looked through the full lot for the dark red 1970 Buick Riviera and found it not far from the entrance. I had to park further away and walk over to the car. A middle-aged man, Hammond I presumed, sat in the car and he was watching the door with barely a blink.

I rapped on the driver's window and he jumped. He rolled down the window with a scowl on his face. I questioned my logic in hurrying without any backup.

"I'm busy lady, go away." He sounded like a three-pack-a-day smoker. His voice was out-of-place with his solid jaw and overall pleasant looks.

"Mr. Ham…"

"I don't want to buy anything, I don't care about your

church, and I don't have any spare change." He began rolling his window up again.

"I'm here about your rival, Mr. Rogers." I blurted out before the window had rolled shut.

He sat ignoring me and watching the restaurant entrance. I walked around to the passenger side and tried the door, it was unlocked. I hopped in and left the door slightly open for a quick exit if I needed it.

"Look, missy…"

"His death is suspicious, and I just thought you'd like to tell your side of the fight you guys had on the reality show." I rushed out before he began yelling or shoved me out of the car.

"I'm on a job toots and why would I want to talk to you in the first place?" His eyes were still on the entrance.

"If you're waiting for somebody, I can help. I can go in and check if the guy is there. In return you can talk to me for a few minutes."

He turned his angry eyes on me, giving me the once over. He didn't seem impressed because his gaze returned to the entrance.

"I figure you won't talk until this job, whatever it is, is over. If I help you, you promise to give me ten minutes. That's all."

I noticed an envelope in his lap as if he needed it close at hand. There was clutter in the back seat, a few paper coffee cups and a bag of takeout, but not bad. Not a pigsty, thank you.

The minutes ticked by and I waited, staring at his profile as he stared at the entrance. It was like a staring contest, and I had always won against Felicia and Loring growing up. I was a champ.

After maybe five minutes of the stare-down, he cracked. "Look missy, I've got to serve this guy with a summons to appear in court. He's slippery and I don't have time for this."

I raised an eyebrow. Serving papers? It wasn't the reality show worthy, high-profile job I had expected.

"Don't knock it, it pays the bills between following cheating spouses you know."

I didn't actually think before I spoke, which I kicked myself for later. "I'll serve him for you, if he's in there that is. No charge. Then we talk, okay?"

"He has slipped away from me three times before. That's why I'm being patient and letting him come to me, so to speak."

"So he knows you and who to look out for. What's he look like?"

"No way, I don't want to have to go through this again because you blow it."

I stared again.

"Okay, I'll be waiting to delay him until you arrive with the summons if he slips out the front." He showed me a photo of a slightly overweight executive looking type, mid to late thirties with thinning hair, and a trimmed beard. He handed me the envelope from his lap and we both got out of the car.

I must be desperate because I hadn't intended to be to so… brazen in talking to Hammond. I especially didn't plan on serving a summons just to question to him.

After my eyes adjusted to the subdued lighting, I saw a

chain restaurant with a western theme and rough wood paneling. It smelled of steaks, seafood, and sawdust. Just as a hostess asked me how many in my party I spotted my victim at the bar. I wasn't sure if his drinking this early was good or bad for me.

I took a seat, leaving one empty between the summonee and myself. I was running through how I would possibly get him to identify himself so I could officially hand him the summons.

"What can I getcha?" The bartender asked. That was such a loaded question; he really should come up with a better opening.

"I'll have whatever he's having. Send him one on me while you're at it." My heart began to pound. The words had come from my mouth, but I never thought of being so forward in my life. This really wasn't like me. *Jeez girl, just breathe. So you are trying to flirt, it won't kill you.*

The bartender looked me up and down, gave a sly grin, glanced at the man, then shrugged his shoulders. *Oh, just shoot me now. I suck at flirting.*

In less than a minute a scotch and soda was plunked down in front of me and my query.

"I didn't order another. At least I don't remember ordering it." His words weren't slurred, but they weren't far from it. The bartender just pointed at me as if he couldn't bring himself to say the words.

I smiled. I tried to give him a sexy smile, but that was a new concept to me and I really should have used time in front of a mirror to get it down. I hope it didn't look more like a grimace.

He just stared at me. Either my smile was scaring him

or he couldn't see clearly already. I didn't want to fail at flirting. I would feel mortified and never let myself live it down.

I winked at him, which was also new to me. I think that went better than my smile, may have even looked like an actual wink and not something in my eye. What was I thinking?

The summonee smiled at me and winked back. *Gulp.* Oh crap, I wanted to run. He slid over to the chair between us and pressed his shoulder against mine. I dug my nails into the glass of scotch and hoped the glass wouldn't shatter.

"Aside from being sexy, what do you do for a living?" he said in a low voice, as if it would make it sound better.

No wonder he was drinking alone in the middle of the day. I bit my tongue to keep from groaning at how terrible it was. Worst. Pickup. Line. Ever.

"I… umm… I'm an event planner. And you?" I had really hoped he would start with names. I'm old-fashioned that way.

"I'm an accountant. It's good work really, pay's crap though." He took a big swig of his drink.

I hadn't touched mine because I planned to return to work. I was never more tempted to drain a glass than at that moment.

"My name's Felicia." My cousin will never know I used her name. It will die with me.

"Steve." His "s" sprayed me. I took a napkin and wiped my face. I didn't even try to hide it. This wasn't going to work.

"Steve Teskeron." More spray. More wiping.

BINGO!

I fished the summons out of my purse and leaned close. In a loud voice, so he would be sure to hear me, I said, "Steve Teskeron, you have been served."

I slapped a twenty on the counter, hoped off the bar stool and fought to walk rather than sprint out.

The door closed on the bartender laughing.

"Did you do it?" Mr. Mike Hammond was waiting at the door. "I hear laughing, that can't be good."

"You hear the bartender laughing at Steve for believing I was coming onto him." I shivered all over. "You owe me twenty dollars for the two drinks I bought."

"Twenty dollars, no way." He yelped.

"Then you owe me some answers, mister."

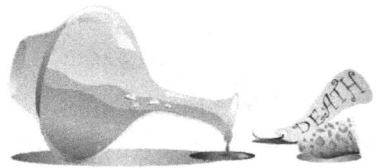

CHAPTER 10

*H*e surveyed me. "Okay, let's go to a fast food place so I can eat and use the boy's room."

I followed his car to a burger place a block away. I admit I didn't trust him to honor the deal now that his summons had been delivered.

The burger joint was a fifties retro themed place with the old-fashioned vinyl booths, laminate and chrome tables, small juke box on each table, black and white checker-board tiled floor, and employees in car hop uniforms. I waited at a table and Hammond joined me with a full tray of food. He handed me a milkshake and fries for helping him out. Wow, big spender.

He barely got the wrapper off the first of his burgers before his mouth was packed full, fries jammed in to fill any empty spaces. I think I could actually hear his arteries hardening and his cholesterol sky rocketing as I watched. As he chewed, and chewed, broken up with an occasional swallow of diet soda, it became clear I would have to ask my questions and hope I could understand his answers around the food.

I explained who I was and my interest with my name found on his dead body. "I need to ask you about Roderick Rogers' death. Can you think of anybody who might have had an issue with him?" I hoped he might be helpful if it appeared I was seeking his insights. It's a start to get him talking.

"Yeah, a lot of people." He said around another mouthful. His words were backed by the oldies tune "Secret Agent Man" which made me think of Liam, of course. The universe was taunting me.

"Could you elaborate on that?"

"Nope, not really." He swallowed and hesitated to take another bite, "Word around the PI community is he was feathering his bed with the knowledge he got on the job."

"I don't understand, what do you mean?" I didn't want vague statements, out with it, mister.

"Well missy, it means he was probably getting paid to keep what he found to himself. You know." He took a big bite of greasy burger followed with more fries crammed in.

"You mean blackmail?" I wanted to be sure what he meant. I had to wait for him to chew and wash it all down with another big swig of diet soda.

"Yes, nail on head honey." His throaty tone was sarcastic.

"What about the fist fight you got into on the show?" I got out before he filled his mouth again.

The music changed and "Jailhouse Rock" was

orchestrating our conversation. Roderick Rogers would probably have ended up in jail if a blackmail victim hadn't stopped his sucking them for money by killing him.

"He was sabotaging me on the show, he was spreading lies about me that was hurting my ability to do my job, but I don't think that got on camera." He took another swallow of diet soda. "He was a cheat and underhanded, but that doesn't mean I'm stupid enough to kill him. Besides, the show producers and director pitted us against each other intending to make it volatile, they even suggested we throw some punches for ratings. I was happy to oblige." He produced a toothpick from his pocket and dug at a few teeth.

"Wouldn't a contract for the reality show have been a windfall? If he was causing you problems, you must have wanted him out of the running." I was careful to keep my tone conversational.

"Oh sure, who wouldn't, that's part of competing. After the fight on camera he told me he didn't care anymore 'cause he had bigger fish on the line than the reality show." He stuffed the remains of his second burger into his bottomless pit and was attacking the remaining fries.

"Did he explain who or what that bigger fish was?" Suspicions were forming in my mind, specifically the sheriff or commissioner.

"Nah, he wouldn't even if we was bosom buddies, now would he?" He turned his attention to his dessert, a banana split.

There was only one last thing to follow up on. "Surely

a name or two comes to mind that could have held a grudge, maybe a case…"

The music changed to "Walking After Midnight" to punctuate our final words. Not only was it a personal favorite but brought visions of Mason to mind.

"Look honey, I told you there were plenty of people. He wasn't liked much by other investigators. He made enemies even with the police and if the rumors are true, he may have used what he found on cases to wrestle money from some poor saps. I don't have names cause it wasn't any of my business."

That seemed to be the end of any answers I could get from Mike Hammond. I felt like my cholesterol level spiked just sitting near him.

I didn't go directly back to work. I needed to know everything I could about the Mike Hammond while I had a chance. So, I followed him.

I never tailed another person before, but the concept is to follow without them realizing it. First, I put sunglasses on and a ball cap from my back seat. I tried to keep several cars between us. At one stoplight, I pulled over to the curb and ducked until the light changed and I pulled out after a bit to continue tailing him. I almost lost him that time.

He made his way into downtown, but on a side street that hadn't been touched by downtown revitalization. I watched him park behind in a small building with Hammond Investigations sign on the front. It sat among several old buildings along the low-rent street.

It was a red brick two story construction. The upper story had a lace curtains and appeared like they lived above their office. That was common in many of the older downtown businesses to have a home above the store. Although, now many upper floors were used as storage or rented out.

I drove around and on the back side there was a small deck off the second floor with two folding chairs and a plastic table with a small Hibachi grill. Yep, he lived here too. He had a prime view of a parking lot for some second hand store, but if he stretched his neck way out, he could catch a glimpse of Pikes Peak. No doubt it was cost effective.

Getting the reality show contract could mean more than just money or status, but a simple home with grass and trees rather than asphalt. Maybe wifey has wanted to garden or have relatives visit which probably can't be done with the seemingly tiny space above their office.

I parked out of sight and ducked into the deli a few doors down with a couple of bistro tables sitting out front and a few larger black metal tables with umbrellas along the side. The deli inside had a long glass case with thirty or more meats and cheeses for slicing and above was a chalk board with sandwiches, sides, and soft drinks to order.

Since I hadn't eaten any of the fries at the fast food place Hammond took me to, I ordered a half a sandwich.

"Hey, I noticed a private investigator a few doors over, is that the guy on the television show?" I tried to break the ice with the skinny kid who took my order. I was suspicious of a skinny deli worker making a decent sand-wich, but it gave me a reason to be here.

"Yeah, you watch it?" He was busy slicing my hard Italian Salami and didn't look up.

"Oh, I've caught a few episodes, you know. I saw where Hammond and the other guy got into a fight. Did you see that one?" I crossed my fingers behind my back.

"Yeah, I saw it. Mr. Hammond was in here the next day talking smack about the guy to my dad. The other guy, Roger something-or-other, he really got under Hammond's skin, like telling him what a hack screw-up wannabe he was and how he was going to be famous and Hammond could eat his dust." He layered my hard salami, slathered it with basil pesto, roasted red peppers, provolone cheese, and lettuce on warmed focaccia bread.

"That's terrible. Was that guy always so cruel?"

He shrugged his shoulders, "I don't know, seemed a bit of a hard ass on the show. But they do things for ratings they probably wouldn't really do, you know. It's not that real, just cheap amateurs." My stomach was growling now.

"Sounds like Hammond took it seriously. Do you think the fight was real then and not just staged for the ratings?" I was giving him the floor to gossip, the least he could do was oblige.

"Oh yeah, Hammond was fuming and so angry he couldn't just let it go. It was real. He even said he could've strangled the jerk with his bare hands if the cameras weren't recording it all." He wrapped my half sandwich up in paper, got my iced tea, added some napkins and bagged it.

"Smells great, thanks." I paid and sat in my car to eat while watching Hammond's place. The sandwich was divine and I would be sending friends and family to this hidden gem. It was much better than a fast-food joint and certainly more my taste.

Seemed Hammond had the motive of revenge or simple smack-down for the vicious words. Maybe he meant to only get Rogers sick as pay back but it reacted on him stronger. Geez, when would people get it through their noggins that words hurt and leave deep wounds?

I made it back to my office just before a hail storm unleashed. I hated to leave my car exposed to the pummeling.

I found several voice mail messages to answer and a number of emails too. I focused on work, but in the back of my mind I kept thinking about the *bigger fish on the line* that Hammond claimed Rogers was excited about. Of course, an affair between the Sheriff and County Commissioner was prime blackmail material. I might find other big fish once I went through his files.

Mid afternoon I realized Liam must have lost interest in assisting now that his father was in town. I imagine they were spending time together. It was for the best all around. He had been helpful wading through all the security video, but I didn't need the personal complications. Thinking of complications reminded me of Mason's sister, Marisa, the talk we had and how she had liked me almost immediately. I could see us becoming friends given time.

I was anxious to get home and begin studying the files Rogers' secretary and business partner had let me borrow. I had three suspects so far, the sheriff, commissioner, and rival Mike Hammond. There may be a standout suspect in the files. I wonder if the police had followed the same line of thought. Surely the police had taken the files, or copies like I had, and were scouring through them.

I was just glad I didn't have Detective Lawrence eyeing me again as the murderer. I forced my attention back to the checklist I was following on the pro golf tournament.

I was wading back into working on a press release when a knock at my door broke my concentration. Liam lounged against the doorframe in tan slacks and a white button-down shirt that accentuated his golden-brown skin. The shirt was unbuttoned a few and the overall look was pure sex appeal. He had to know it, too.

His eyes leveled a challenge to me. He wasn't playing fair. I caught a whiff of his cologne, a different scent from yesterday. It was more sweet and sensual, spice like patchouli and musk for an exotic yet rich scent.

"Sorry I had some business to deal with while it was early enough in London. How is the sleuthing going?" So much for Liam moving on or being with his dad. His comment confirmed he looked at this as more fun and less serious. I suppose when you deal with national security and terrorist threats every day a run-of-the-mill murder was lighter fare.

But I was aware of the risks when on the trail of a killer. All I needed this time around was to understand the connection between the resort and Rogers well enough to explain why he had my name with him when he died.

He clearly had been working a case for somebody that had him following the sheriff and commissioner. Perhaps it was one of their spouses. Plus, the rival private investigator was a suspect but, he had no connection to the resort that I could tell. I wondered if Rogers' was onto something big that would pay substantially besides the sheriff. If he supplemented his income with hush money, then somebody could have killed him to eliminate a financial drain and threat. Those files might point to a likely victim.

"Of course, and you've been neglecting Ariya I'm told. I don't want your taking time away from family on my conscious." I tried not to look at him, but I couldn't pull my eyes away. Really. *Talk about eye candy.*

"Ariya may want to see me, but I get the impression that I'm not so welcome by Mr. Garrett. I think it's my employment. Some people don't handle it well, think I'm spying on them personally or something." He shared this glimpse into his life without hesitation. "I wish she wasn't staying with them until after the wedding."

I wasn't sure if I wanted to know the details of Liam Rajesh Bryan. At first he seemed a persistent flirt, then helpful flirt, after the flirtation had ramped up a notch to the kiss on the cheek I saw him as wanting something. I wasn't sure just what he wanted. I mean other than the obvious thing all men want from a woman. He was up to something.

He held my eyes in a steady gaze, "I wanted to work on those files this evening with you, but I've actually been summoned to a dinner party at the Garrett home. Since I've been scarce, I should attend." His hungry eyes made it very clear he wanted time alone with me, but again I wondered what was his real motivation.

"I'll start in on the files myself tonight, so don't worry

about it." I still hadn't taken my eyes from him and vice versa. There was definite electricity in the air and if one of us didn't flinch soon I didn't want to think of what it would be like when the electricity exploded.

A throat being cleared broke our charged staring match. Liam moved aside and Chad stood behind him.

"Julienne, I'm leaving a little early but I'll be in tomorrow at seven to cover a few things." Chad gave me a direct look that served as a reminder about getting involved with guests. He turned that look to Liam.

"What was that about? He's never been hostile to me before." He no longer looked hungry, but amused.

"Resort policy that staff, all staff, aren't to fraternize with the guests." My eyes were now free to look at the paperwork on my desk, or at my computer screen, even my phone, but not directly in his eyes again.

"I see. Seems I should've found another hotel after all. Because I'm not giving up on you until I absolutely have to catch a plane."

He was determined; I'd give him that. The phone rang at that moment and I gave a startled jump from the pent up tension. He didn't move to leave when I answered, which I had hoped he would.

"Oh, hi Aunt Regina. What's up?"

"We're making dinner tonight for you. What do you want, my Chicken Florentine Crepes or my leftover pot roast?" It was clear from her tone I couldn't refuse.

"Your pot roast sounds great Auntie." I knew when to give in gracefully, plus she hated "auntie." But I was suspicious about what prompted this visit until I remembered only a few hours ago trying to recruit my cousin to help me. Felicia no doubt told her mother.

"Should I stop on the way home and pick anything up?"

"Yes, we'll need plenty of wine with Lars and Loring. You never have enough on hand for those two. Get some bread too."

I hung up and found Liam had been watching me the whole time.

"I guess you've got family plans from the sound of it. I really wanted to spend the evening with you even if that meant pouring through files and eating take out." He shrugged slightly.

"We both have family time tonight. I'll see you tomor-row, maybe." I wanted to go over those files myself since Chad already wanted the Sheriff and Commissioner issue kept from him. It was best all around to cut this short.

He started to turn, then stopped and faced me, "It's the kiss, isn't it? I won't apologize, it wasn't completely unwanted and only on the cheek." A hint of a smile flitted across his lips, "I suspect you're more afraid because you're tempted." His eyes bore into me.

Did he do interrogations? Because he was a whole new level of man than I'd ever encountered before and he played hardball.

"I guess you'll never know, but your temporary status is definitely two strikes against you." I tried for a matching hint of a smile.

"My offer still stands, that is far more permanent." He still stood at the door, but his presence and cologne enveloped me.

"That won't be permanent either, I plan on managing several resorts around the world, not just London. When I move on, I doubt you'll follow." I turned to my computer.

He took two small steps closer, but I couldn't breathe. I stayed focused on my computer screen, oblivious to what was on the display.

"You aren't a nun and you can't shut yourself off because you'll move around a bit." He walked out leaving me staring ahead.

This was the one big hitch in my plans. Mason fit with my plans, at least I thought he had. He could take photos anywhere in the world and he made it clear he had no problem traveling alongside me. At the moment, I felt that was an empty hope that would only end up breaking my heart.

CHAPTER 11

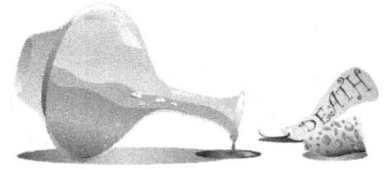

I made it home before my Aunt and the family descended on me, even with stopping at the liquor store and bakery for a dozen croissants. I settled in my second bedroom turned into my home office. It was larger than my work office, and far more comfortable. I had just one window that looked out onto my front, nice plush carpeting, colorful artwork gifted to me from my Uncle's art gallery, a nice desk with my desktop computer and a locking file cabinet.

I settled into my ergonomic chair and glanced through the files enough to make notes of the date, name of the client, and the purpose of hiring him. Peggy Faire had given me the last twelve months of jobs, I would have to thank her for that. I knew full well she entrusted them to me and I took that seriously.

I knew family was in the house when the noise level immediately spiked as if raiding hordes had invaded. They had keys as my backup and it wasn't unusual for them to show up unannounced to make dinner.

Aunt Regina was in the kitchen getting dishes down and Felicia and Loring were arguing, again… still… always. They were the epitome of siblings in their spats, yet they would fight anybody outside the family for even looking cross-eyed at the other. One time, I had to stop Felicia from keying the car of Loring's ex-girlfriend who viciously dumped him and I talked Loring out of fighting a man who got too hands-on when Felicia waited tables one summer.

A knock at my door pulled me from the files, "Julienne, ma cher, come join us." Uncle Lars was a gentle soul who owned an art gallery in the municipality of Manitou Springs that is adjacent to the western side of Colorado Springs. He is middle aged with distinguished graying temples amidst black hair and gentle soft brown eyes.

The town of Manitou Springs is funky, a little-bit hippy, and tourist driven and Lar's art gallery features around twenty artists with styles from mixed media, watercolor, acrylics, and classic oil paintings. I love the watercolors so that's what is featured in my home most.

"Be right there. Merci mon cher oncle." I would slip into French occasionally with them, a habit they encouraged.

I carefully gathered the files plus the notes I'd made and locked them up in the desk drawer. I'd go over them more after my family was gone. But, now I had to face the inevitable grilling if Felicia had snitched on me as I suspected.

I joined the four of them around the dinner table that had place mats and matching napkins set out. As always, a place was fully set at the end of the table but left vacant. That was our tribute to my mother who died when I was just twelve of breast cancer. I had bought four bottles of wine and two of them were already opened and on the table.

The wine bottles were passed around first, priorities were clear in the family, then the salad, the almond green beans, and finally the leftover pot roast that had a distinct French Onion flavor I loved. They didn't wait long; the food was still being passed when the questions began.

"So, I hear you're poking around about that guy on the news who died in his car and caused a wreck." Aunt Regina had no fear, especially since she considered herself my surrogate mother.

I took a breath, but didn't get a word out before Uncle Lars jumped in, "How long did your bruises take to heal after the last time you looked into a murder? It was a good month from my reckoning. That's quite enough."

I glared at cousin Felicia. That was the last time I offered to include her in my sleuthing efforts. I made the motions of loading an invisible slingshot and shooting her between the eyes. *Why is it family can reduce you to a child again?*

"Don't blame her for your gallivanting around." Aunt Regina was getting warmed up, "It's as though you want to taunt a criminal, like you enjoy the brush with danger and a killer. Girls in my day were married and raising children not chasing after psycho…" She realized what she had said and stopped.

My mouth was full of meatloaf, but my eyes met hers. I swallowed. This was an old argument in my family. I thought we had moved past the having children expectation. There wasn't a sound. Lars and Loring were fascinated with their food because they knew I wouldn't listen to them in this, Felicia's eyes were as big as... dinner plates, and Aunt Regina had closed her eyes and shook her head.

I took a big gulp of wine. I didn't want to have an argument over this yet again. My Aunt opened her eyes, and I saw deep regret floating with tears.

She cleared her throat and began again with a softer voice, "Of course times have changed, but my fear for your safety doesn't change." Her eyes asked that I let it go, she had slipped and was sorry.

I cleared my throat from the mixed emotions that had lodged there, "Times have indeed changed, but I hope to never lose your love." A truce was in place. "I had asked for somebody to join me so I wasn't taking any undo risks. I'm only trying to clear up the connection with the resort to protect its reputation."

I took a breath for the next part, "Plus, the deceased had my business card on him and that unbearable Detective Lawrence visited me immediately. I'd like to know why a PI had my card." The mention of the detective would help them to back off a bit after his single-minded pursuit of me as a killer last fall.

"Did he accuse you again?" My Aunt's eyes flashed lightning.

"Call that lawyer, your dad will pay for it." My Uncle.

"I thought the guy had a heart attack." My cousin Loring contributed.

Felicia kept her big mouth shut since she knew we weren't okay yet.

I explained how PI Roderick Rogers had apparently been poisoned and the police hadn't asked me any more questions after a guest vouched for me. I probably should have figured out a way to avoid Liam's involvement.

"A guest? Why would a guest be involved?" Uncle Lars jumped on that like the last glass of wine in a bottle of Opus.

"This guest must be somebody pretty important to sway that ogre Detective." Aunt Regina was back in fighting form and was trying to wrestle the answer out of me with her eyes alone.

"It's not... he's not anybody, I mean... he's..." What do you call MI5, law enforcement? Special Security – for a foreign country? I sputtered to a stop and was now evaluating my food.

Felicia chose this moment to break her silence, "Oh my god, she likes him. Whoever he is, she likes the guy."

I lifted my head just enough to pin her with my glare. She was batting a thousand today. I would get even if it took me the rest of my life.

I needed to change the subject, my mind frantically searched for something. "Have you guys ever heard of Mike Hammond, Donald Guy, or ummmm Gloria Vanders?" I resorted to names associated with Rogers.

"Don't change the subject. Who is this guest that helped you with the Detective and be quick about it Julienne Atsila LaMere." Oh no, she never used my middle name because it's Cherokee after my maternal grandmother.

For the second time during dinner it became quiet.

"He's a guest from England, and he is... you have to swear not to tell anybody else. He works for MI5. You can't tell anybody that." I looked at Felicia who motioned zipping her lips and throwing away the key. I then glared at Loring.

"How are you involved with a spy now? How is this possible? Please tell me you aren't actually interested in him." This outburst was from Uncle Lars who never took an assertive role in these arguments.

"I'm coordinating his sister's wedding that he's attending, and he stopped by my office when the detective started in on me. He showed his credentials and vouched for me. Chad has him helping me with the private detective's death. Which is a good thing since the police told him it was poison." I was babbling like an idiot. Just shoot me now.

I poured myself another glass of wine and took a big gulp. This evening wasn't going as I'd hoped. If Mason were here, he could charm my Aunt and reassure my Uncle.

"Wait, what were those names again?" Aunt Regina for the last minute save with a change of topic and winner of my gratitude.

"Ummm, Hammond, Donald Guy, and Dr. Gloria Vanders." The only names I could remember from the files because one was so different and the other was close to Vanderbilt.

"Lars, remember that pretentious woman who had more money than taste that wanted you to acquire a painting for her and she would pay you a commission? That was her, this Dr. Vanders person."

Often I forget how Colorado Springs and adjacent Manitou may be just under half-a-million people but it's more like a small town in attitudes and feel. This was one of those prime examples.

"What do you know about her?" I tried to slip it in without sparking the argument about my inquiring mind.

"She's some specialist hot shot, I think it was thyroid or something. She's pushy, a real know-it-all who wanted art as an investment. And if I've taught you anything about art…" Uncle Lars didn't finish.

The rest of us recited in unison, "It under-performs the stock market and isn't recession proof."

I pushed my surprise aside, "Was she with her husband?" Which, if I remembered the notes I took, was the subject of Rogers' investigation.

"Oh yeah, the two of them were oil and water. I can't imagine they'll last long." Aunt Regina filled her glass with more wine and grabbed the croissants.

"I bet there was a prenup. Only reason I can imagine that he stayed with such a nasty tempered woman." Uncle Lars shot off as he retrieved the dessert, Aunt Regina's signature Orange-Cardamom Madeleines.

I needed to run the name by Nathan who still ran in the medical circles. He might be able to get me more scoop on both her and the hubby. I should look online for photos in case one of them was on the security videos. I needed to go through those files in more detail.

"Now, about this Englishman…"

The evening finally wound down and my family left,

but not before I had to promise I wasn't interested in Liam. Uncle Lars grudgingly admitted that maybe somebody of his experience might be good for my safety. I didn't explain how he wasn't an actual agent, it would have just prolonged my misery.

I jumped on my computer to see if Nathan was available to Skype. When I was snowbound in a mountain resort with a killer a few months ago, I was surprised to find Nathan Skyping me. He gives me reports regularly on how he is keeping in touch with his grandchildren that way.

He didn't seem to be active at the moment, so I took a chance and put a call through via the video chat program. He didn't answer and the video call hung up after so many rings. I was about to shut down for the night when I got Nathan video calling me. I accepted the call.

"Howdy neighbor, I didn't know how to answer your call on this program, so I just waited to call you. What's up?" He had the camera angled too much and I could only see the top of his head.

"I need an assistant in my investigation, think you're up for it?" I kept my tone carefree so he didn't feel any pressure to help.

"You bet your sweet bippy I am. So am I Watson?" He moved closer to the camera, His eyes came into view.

"Watson? Oh, sure. Except I'm no Sherlock."

"What's my assignment Holmes?" His voice was downright peppy, exuberant even.

"I need you to find out the gossip, just the gossip, from your doctor and nurse friends about Dr. Gloria Vanders. Specifically anything about her possibly hiring the dead

PI." That was a well-defined task, hopefully he wouldn't go off script.

"Gossip only, why she might have hired a private dick. Got it." He nodded his head, at least I think that's what he was doing. The angle made it look funny.

"Before you take off, I hear you've got another handsome young man in your life. When do we get to meet him and give our feedback on him?"

I was going to have a stern talk with Delores. "That's not going to happen. I have my family harassing me over my love life, or lack of one, so I really don't need you guys interfering."

"That's not fair deary, we're only looking out for our girl."

I knew he meant well, but I had to draw the line and stick to it. "Nope. Not happening. And tell Delores she's got a whole lot of explaining to do."

I disconnected the video call and got the files out for another look-see. I figured I had about an hour before I dropped from exhaustion. Somehow I needed to find a source to get information about the sheriff and commissioner. Wait a minute, where was that file? It wasn't among these files.

Why wouldn't there be a file on the Sheriff Morrison and Commissioner Gage? Maybe it was new, and he kept it in his desk rather than the file cabinet, or Peggy Faire knew how explosive that case was in this town and feared my leaking it to the press or something. There was the possibility he wasn't formally hired by a spouse to get evidence of an affair, but he was tailing them for his own reasons.

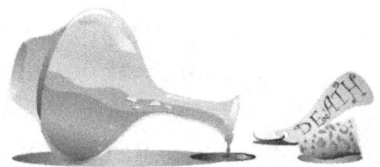

CHAPTER 12

I had dreams of serving a summons to appear in divorce court most of the night. I was tucking those away in my memory for the next time I ranted about my job. Not that I do that but rarely.

I left myself a list after studying Rogers' files last night. The first item was to call Peggy and find out about Rogers' case where he was following the sheriff and commissioner.

I briefly considered putting Peggy on the list of suspects, she had leant him money just to keep the business going and she had easy access to slip him poison. But despite that I couldn't see her as the killer. But I didn't completely rule it out. Which is why the missing file on the Sheriff and Commissioner job seemed to point to Peggy too.

I wanted to look up any social media on Dr. Gloria Vanders and this Donald Guy to see if I recognized them from the security tapes I resigned myself to the fact I had to either watch all the tapes Liam had, or ask Liam if they looked familiar. But before all that, I wanted to swing by Rogers' office and see if Peggy Faire knew anything about the missing file.

I drove by the six red brick offices in the strip mall, and only Rick Rogers had the lights on at the early hour of seven in the morning. There was no movement as I drove past. Maybe Peggy Faire was boxing up his office in the back.

I parked in the side lot with one other car and the weeds growing in every crack in the asphalt. The silver two door compact must be Peggy's. I found the office door was locked, probably too early for her usual hours.

I knocked, "Peggy, it's Julienne. I was here yesterday, remember?" No answer.

I peeked through the large picture window. The lights were on but there was no sign of anybody around. Maybe she forgot to turn the lights off when she left yesterday. I tried knocking until my knuckles hurt and gave up. I would call her and set a time to come by and talk with her.

It took longer than I expected to get to work; I had hit the rush hour traffic. When I finally arrived, I sat in the employee parking and phoned Rogers' office. There was no answer so it went to voicemail. I guess if I was the only employee and maybe looking for another PI, I might come in late to the office. That seemed the likely reason she wasn't answering. I left a message for her to call me and walked to my office. I forgot all about phoning her again as my duties took over.

Mid morning I took a few moments to search for Dr. Vanders and her husband online. There was a LinkedIn with no profile picture. Her Facebook had some photos of social events at least. I printed a photo out of both her and her husband for reference. While I was there I looked at the rest of her photos since the security profile allowed me to look. She attended some swanky parties all right. I hoped Nathan could find some information on her.

I tried for Donald Guy, but there wasn't a social media profile of any kind. Okay. He was going to be the problem child, I could tell already.

I looked up Sheriff Leland Morrison and then Commissioner Shannon Gage. They both had personal pages with tight security, but they were also on their respective department's Facebook pages. Not much there to glean.

I needed to stretch my legs, so I took a walk to the pro golf shop to discuss promotional items for the LPGA Tournament they will need to order for their shop.

I was returning to my office when Liam met me walking through the lobby. The lobby always took my breath away with its stained glass ceiling lit from behind and the white marble tile floor with inlaid gold marble in the image of the sun's rays.

I gave an inward sigh which made me question why a handsome man showing me attention annoyed me. He was a complication in my life that presented problems I answered. His job offer was a case in point.

"Hey love, I've time today to help out. Have you looked though those files yet? I could help with that." He wore jeans today and an azure blue dress shirt which made me appreciate his style, and the overall... okay, he looked *fine* from top to bottom.

"I ummm. I've looked through the files, but I'm busy today, plus there's that little wedding rehearsal and the dinner this afternoon I believe you're expected to attend." I hoped he would have lost interest by now since his dad was in town and this was all just a diversion for him, including myself.

"Right you are. The rehearsal." He snapped his fingers, "Which reminds me, apparently Mrs. Garrett is quite the flower grower, they want to bring fresh-cut flowers for the centerpieces at the dinner. Would that be okay?" He had slowly moved closer until he was in easy reach.

"I'll call Ariya and discuss the details, but we can probably work with it." I moved to continue walking, but he placed his hand gently on my arm.

"I know I was cheeky and things are awkward now. You're putting distance between us. But, I'd like to help out for the next couple of hours."

I relented, I could use the help and I knew it. "Okay, there is something you could look into."

I unlocked my office and had just settled into my chair when Detective Lawrence exited Chad's office.

"Ms. LaMere, I need to talk to you again." He did a double take when he saw Liam lounging in my visitor chair.

"I have a busy day, can this wait?" I couldn't keep the slight hostile tone from creeping into my voice. *Steady LaMere.*

"Mr. Bryan, if you'll excuse us." But Liam didn't move, and I was grateful for his presence now. The detective waited a few heartbeats and then ignored Liam's refusal to leave. "Why did you call Peggy Faire this morning?"

I scrunched my forehead, "Why are you asking?" I really wasn't in the mood.

"Because she was found this morning in her office murdered, and yet again you are somehow involved." He crossed his arms.

I had no words. I liked the feisty Peggy. Then it sank in that she might have been inside when I was knocking, dying or dead already. What if I had arrived earlier, would I have seen the killer? Could the killer have still been inside when I was knocking? I sank my head in my hands and took several deep breaths to hide just how shaken I was. Without lifting my head I asked, "How?"

"Poison again from the looks of it, same vomit and such. How did you know her?" His voice had taken an edge.

Liam answered before I could even think of what to say, "We both met Ms. Faire the day before yesterday when we visited to ask why the detective would have Ms. LaMere's business card. She was pleasant, and we both found her a lovely lady."

My heart swelled for his taking the lead even though I could have answered for myself. I wasn't sure if I could have been so... articulate. I would've babbled because I was shaken. I wouldn't share I was at the office this morning either since I had zero useful information to provide.

I lifted my head to show them both there were no tears, just a sadness for the waste of life.

"Where were you between six and eight this morning?"

"At home, in bed then getting ready for work."

"Anybody verify that?" The detective narrowed his eyes. I could swear Liam held his breath.

"No, I was alone." I kept my eyes on the detective, but from the corner of my eye I saw Liam let out a breath.

"You left a message asking for a missing file. What would that be?" His jaw clenched, and he had fire in his eyes.

I held my hand up to stop Liam from answering for me, "I believe Rogers may have been around here surveilling somebody for a job. When we met her, she gave us copies of the last few cases he was working on. I couldn't see any connection to the resort, so I called her thinking there must be a file missing."

"You aren't an investigator, private or otherwise, so you are interfering…." He was turning red in the face and I had visions of myself in jail for trying to save the resort's reputation. Talk about above and beyond my duties.

Liam cut him off, "She isn't interfering in your investigation. She received copies of files from the co-owner of the business. That was completely up to Ms. Faire. Your access to the original files hasn't been hindered or tampered with." Liam bulldozed through Detective Lawrence's indignation.

"I better not find you snooping around, or you'll see a jail cell for interfering in an investigation." He stormed out.

I flirted with calling the lawyer that helped me last fall. Not just yet.

Chad joined Liam and I as soon as the detective left. At this rate I needed a bigger work office to handle all the visitors. The air was getting stuffy from so many warm bodies in the small space, or maybe I should say so much hot air with Detective Lawrence's visit.

"My wanting to clear the resort has gotten you in trouble with Lawrence. I never meant for that to happen." Chad crossed his arms.

"I don't think I'm in trouble at this point. But, he's not happy with me, that's clear."

Chad turned to Liam, "I know I have no right asking, but can we impose upon you…"

"I'm more than happy to work on this with Julienne, night and day. Except for when wedding duties call." He looked directly in my eyes as he answered Chad.

"Julie, you can fill him in on what you have so far. Well, I'll let you two get back to it, then." He turned and left, happy to distance himself, no doubt.

I could kick Chad. Hard. He didn't indicate if that meant to tell Liam about the Sheriff and Commissioner dalliance. I decided Chad's open-ended *fill him in* was permission to share everything.

I ran through what I had found out about the County Sheriff and Commissioner, plus my talk with the rival detective on the reality show. I withheld my morning visit to Rogers' office. He raised an eyebrow but said nothing. I couldn't tell if his surprise was over the progress I made without him or that I kept it from him.

I handed him the photo I'd printed out of Dr. and

Mr. Vanders. "The woman hired Rogers about six months ago thinking hubby there was unfaithful. I hadn't found any photos anywhere online of Donald Guy." I let everything sink in for a few moments.

"She looks familiar." He looked up at me, "I'm sure I saw her in one of the security videos."

I hadn't expected that so fast, guess his training was coming in handy after all. I unlocked my file cabinet and took out the DVDs. They were still separated into two piles, one for each of us and had the notes we left notes on Post-its.

"Any guess which one?"

He took out the two labeled Lake Patio and handed them to me. Within minutes we were scanning through the video again, only this time he stood next to my chair, our heads were nearly touching as we watched the fast motion activity. The electricity between us was even more pronounced, but I pushed that aside.

"I think this might be the spot, slow down, please." His voice was low in my ear. *Gulp.*

After a few minutes, he pointed to the screen. "There, that's her. I'm positive."

I squinted at the screen and then looked at the printed photo. There was a definite resemblance, but the camera angle of her face as she sat at a patio table was in profile. We kept watching and eventually she turned her head to face the camera for a few seconds. I paused the video, grabbed a screen shot, and copied it into a document with the day and time typed in.

The recording continued, and we saw Roderick Rogers walk past her. She jumped up and followed him a few steps where they got into an argument. After a good minute of her poking him in the chest and him talking with his hands in angry gestures, one of our security personnel broke it up. I backed the recording up and grabbed another screen shot of the two arguing and copied to the document noting that time.

"I think I know that security man." After a quick phone call to security I found the man, Darrel, was working today. I asked if they could radio him to stop by for some questions.

Darrel knocked on my open door five minutes later. He was a big man, well over six feet tall. He stayed just outside my doorway after looking over the tiny office space. I handed him the document I printed with the screen captures over my desk and he leaned across the threshold to take it. "Can you remember anything about what they were arguing about? It's important. That man died a few days ago and the police have been asking us about him."

He pulled out a small notebook and flipped through it. "Here it is, she was yelling that she wanted her money back."

"Like he didn't do a good job sort of thing?" I wanted to be crystal clear what was said.

"Well, not so much that. She yelled something about her husband paying to keep it quiet and she was the one who hired him. It sounded like he got in the middle of marital problems."

That would fit if he was getting hush money from the husband who probably got the money from his wife to begin with. But how smart was it to go against the wealthy and socially connected Dr. Gloria Vanders? That could have gotten him killed all right.

"Did she threaten him?"

"She told him there would be no more money from her husband, but I didn't hear an outright threat."

There wasn't much else, so Darrel went back to his assigned area.

"Hammond told you Rogers was blackmailing people. That fits with Dr. Vanders' argument." Liam treated this differently after hearing of Peggy's murder, more seriously.

"But how did she know Rogers would be here? Peggy had to have directed her here." I thought aloud.

"Sure, she could've thought it was about another job and Vanders would only talk to Rogers."

I had done the same thing essentially to talk to Hammond. It made sense. Rogers was spending so much time at the resort and Vanders was already a client so Peggy probably didn't think it was a problem.

"Okay, Peggy doesn't realize what's really happening and directs Vanders to the resort. She waits until she spots him and then confronts him. But this was the day before he was poisoned."

We returned to scanning all the way until we saw where I was escorting Liam, Jason the groom, and Landon the groom's father back from the tour. We knew Rogers was dead by then. There wasn't anybody obvious hanging around that we could connect to Rogers. Of course, we didn't know what Donald Guy looked like yet.

I checked the time, coming up on lunchtime. I couldn't justify running home to talk to the Nathan about what he might have discovered about Dr. Vanders. Not with the wedding rehearsal and dinner fast approaching and I had only asked for his help last night.

I motioned for Liam to close my office door as I dialed Nathan on the hotel phone and put it on speaker.

"Nathaniel Fitzel, don't waste my time with a sales pitch." He sounded older than I thought of him, but just as cantankerous.

"Nathan, it's Julie…" I began, but didn't get far.

"Oh good, glad you rang me up dear. I called several of my nurse friends. They're ever so helpful, especially lovely Brandy." His voice got younger as he spoke.

I covered my face with my hands as Liam chuckled.

"Nathan, did you find out anything useful? About Dr. Vanders, that is?"

"Oh, you in a hurry or something? That handsome Brit fella Delores met keeping you busy?" Nathan chuckled at his own angling for information.

I, however, looked at the ceiling. I could feel my face turning bright red. "Nathan, you're on speaker phone and I'm not alone."

"Oh, is the Brit there? Don't be shy, son. Speak up, what's your name."

I sent a prayer up to any force in the universe powerful enough to shut Nathan up.

"Mr. Fitzel, I'm Liam Bryan. We're hoping you can help us with any information on Dr. Vanders." Despite his professional tone, his eyes were full of laughter as he watched my every move.

"I'll get to that, but first tell me your intentions towards Julienne."

"That's enough, Nathan. I won't have you screening the men in my life."

Liam cocked his head and quirked an eyebrow up. Okay, poor choice of words. He wasn't exactly *in my life*.

"Mr. Fitzel, I'm only here visiting my sister, but I've seen a kindred spirit in Ms. LaMere and have proposed a way for her to join me in London and still pursue her career. So my intentions are most honorable."

I went from embarrassed to angry, spitting and sputtering angry.

"Julie, I can practically hear the steam coming out of your ears over the phone. He humored an old man and showed he cares about you. Nothing wrong with that. Now, Brandy is the nurse I mentioned." He paused to cough.

"Well Brandy has a good friend who works in Vanders' office. Hubby Vincent made passes at every woman in the office, but they're all afraid to say anything because of Gloria's wrath, which is mighty Brandy's friend says. Anyways, about seven or eight months back Gloria began grousing around the office about how she knew he was stepping out, dipping his wick…"

"We got the idea, Nathan. Get on with it."

"Brandy's friend heard her setting an appointment with a private investigator. Everybody in the office knew she hired somebody to follow Vincent."

"Why didn't she just divorce him? Was there a prenup?" I had to ask, despite how I wanted the call to end quickly.

"Well, nobody's sure. But that's what everyone in the

office figures. Seems Vanders has family money on top of what she makes as some big shot Doc."

"Thanks, Nathan. That was helpful. I got to go."

He tried to get Liam talking again, but I kept putting him off until he finally hung up.

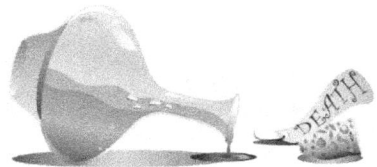

CHAPTER 13

I brought the files with me today, hoping to have enough spare time to go through them in more detail. Chad bought us Sub sandwiches so we could devote every moment on the files.

"You mentioned to the Detective a file might be missing, what file would that be?" Liam had just finished his sandwich.

"There is no file on the couple Rogers was following around the Resort. I imagine somebody hired him, so I called Peggy to ask if there might be a file missing." I drained my cold coffee.

Liam leaned back in his chair with his arms spread and hands behind his head, "Were you ever going to tell me you discovered who the couple was?"

I hoped he would have forgotten or let that go. Today was not my day.

"That information could damage this resort, so Chad asked me not to tell a soul. So, no, I wasn't going to tell you. But, Chad gave his permission when he asked you to help and for me to brief you."

He gazed at me, not in a heated or sexually aware way but part evaluation and part surprised. "Have you ever thought of another career?"

"No, this is my dream job, there isn't any other career I want." I had fought hard for it, too. This management training program had two-hundred-and-fifty applicants, but I was the only one who had worked at the resort for several years already and had a good working relationship with others.

Then the implication of what he was asking struck me like cold water in the face, "Oh no, not covert spy stuff. Not for me, no way." I shook my head so my hair flew about me face.

"I think you would be good at small jobs, plant a few bugs or hand off a document." He smiled like he was making plans.

"Stop thinking about it right now. I want nothing to do with your spook world. Do you understand me?" I felt as though this was the real Liam, a spymaster in the making looking to recruit useful people. I mentally gasped. That was probably why he could offer me a job at a London resort; it was for British Secret Service not so much him personally.

"Oh, I hear you. Still…"

"Let's get back to the files." I shut him down. The thought he offered me a London resort job more for small covert jobs on behalf of MI5 rather than a romantic gesture was like a bucket of ice on my head.

I turned my back on him and kept going through the

files I had. After we scrutinized each of the files and jotted down some notes, we went over them.

"I had Dr. Vanders as a likely suspect, but there's not much new about her. But I noticed numbers tallied on the back of the initial investigation questionnaire." I showed the notations to him.

He quickly flipped through his files, "I have the same thing in Donald Guy's file too. Nobody else's though."

"What do you make of that?" I had my guess, but I didn't want him sizing me up for spy work, so he could share his ideas first.

"It looks like a short date and then a dollar amount. I think this was his log of the hush money the person paid him." Liam shook his head, "It was only a matter of time before somebody tired of paying or eliminated the threat hanging over their head."

That was my assessment too, I just nodded but kept my mouth shut.

"Looks like you picked the two most likely people already. I didn't find any others that had these notations or seemed candidates for blackmail. You have a knack for this." He was trying to catch my eye.

I ignored the comment. "How much was Donald Guy paying him?"

"The notations show three hundred and fifty dollars a month. Small amount, but he was getting money illegitimately for a false insurance claim. He was supposed to be nearly bed ridden and unable to work from the slip and fall at his computer manufacturing job. Rogers followed him to a roofing job where he got paid under the table."

"I think these notations imply Vincent Vanders was

paying two thousand a month to keep Rogers from turning over the explicit photos he took of Vincent… dipping his wick… in what looks like a back room of an office with a much younger gal." I didn't even try to keep the contempt from my voice. I was rooting for Gloria after seeing the photos in the file. Sheesh, he didn't even spring for a decent hotel room.

"Then there is the missing file on the two county public servants. You don't suppose…" He began.

"That Peggy picked up the blackmailing where Rogers left off and it got her killed?" I finished the thought.

I slapped a hand over my mouth and a smug smile spread across his face. Oh no, I was finishing his sentences besides adding to his belief I was low-level spy material.

"It's bloody great conjecture, but without the file, or maybe following them, what can we achieve?" Liam crossed his arms.

"The file will tell us who hired Rogers and might tell us if they were being blackmailed." I crossed my arms too. "Without that we don't have much." I hated to admit it.

"Why don't we turn over what we have on the county officials having an affair to the police? We can make copies of the video surveillance." He raised one eyebrow in challenge.

We might be at a dead end.

The phone rang and I raised an index finger in signal to give me a minute.

"Colorado Springs Resort, how may I help you?"

"It's Tiffany, remember me? I just wanted to tell you

to check the paper, you're in it again." A snotty and smug voice sang out. She hung up before I could say a word.

Tiffany Davidson was a girl in high school who blames me for a guy standing her up but now uses her position at the local paper to make my life difficult. I forgot about Chad's warning that the paper would cover the murder.

I swallowed and slowly replaced the phone receiver to the base. My stomach had rocks weighting it down. Oh no, not again.

"What is it?" Liam's eyebrows scrunched and his eyes filled with concern.

I didn't say anything but bolted from my office toward the lobby where the paper is available for guests to read. I could hear Liam following behind me.

I didn't see any papers around, but a customer service representative at the check-in desk waved me over.

"We collected them as soon as we realized the article was in it." Her voice was conspiratorial.

"How bad?" I forced the words out.

"What're we talking about, please?" Liam asked.

"You haven't seen it yet?" She reached under the desk and plopped a paper down on the raised desk surface. "It's on page three."

I walked to a lobby chair and read through the article with Liam reading over my shoulder. The grandeur of the lobby faded away as I read. Tiffany dedicated one entire paragraph to my card found on Rogers' body and then dredging up how I was a suspect in Pastor Tom Drake's murder last fall. I felt like a deflated balloon when

I finished reading it. Today felt like the universe was ganging up on me.

Liam took the paper from me, folded it back up and returned it to the check-in desk. He escorted me back to my office and led me to my office chair. All I could think was how Rogers' shady dealings and murder would get me fired. Liam faced me, placed his hands on my chair armrests and leaned over to where his face was only inches from mine.

"That settles that. We can't stop now. We've got to remove all suspicion from you and the resort. It's the only way. The sooner the better." He looked at his watch, "But I've got the rehearsal in an hour and a half then I've got the dinner."

The last thing I wanted was people at the rehearsal eyeing me, sizing me up for a murderer.

"Nobody will think of that article because the focus is on Ariya and a happily ever after. Don't worry." When I looked into his eyes, I could see his determination, not worry or even consolation.

"We Brits have an expression, stiff upper lip. During World War II when London was getting air raids and bombed into rubble by the Luftwaffe, the town was covered with posters everywhere reminding people to 'Keep calm and carry on.' That's what we have to do, what you have to do." His pep talk reminded me that people had gone through far worse than what I was experiencing.

It helped. I drew back my shoulders and took a deep fortifying breath.

"You need to check in with Ariya and get ready for

the rehearsal. Don't worry, I'll be fine and I'll be there." I wanted to be alone to think for a while. Although once he left, the small space seemed so empty.

I stared at the framed retro travel poster of Villa D'Este Lake Como in Italy surrounded by the Alps over my desk. It was the shock of the article sprung on me like that. But, why hadn't Chad told me, why hadn't my family called?

I checked my phone and realized I had silenced it while we were going through the videos again for Dr. Vanders. I had three messages, one from Uncle Lars, one from Porsche, and one from Brandon. Brandon was the boyfriend before Mason who was best friends with my cousin Loring and nearly a family member.

His message nearly brought me to tears, "Julie, pay no attention to Tiffany and that article. She's grasping at straws to make trouble for you. I already called her editor and complained. If you need anything, well… call me, okay?"

Sweet Brandon. He was a good guy, just not for me. He would be happy in a rural small town working a factory job and raising a slew of kids. I wanted to see the world and had no desire for children and didn't see that changing – ever. I hoped Brandon got everything he wanted.

I texted everyone in a blanket message that I just found out about the article and was shocked, but I was okay.

I grabbed my notebook and flipped through my notes, refreshing myself on the details, and then I looked at the photos I took at Rogers' office. I was scouring the details of the photos. He had a credenza file cabinet and several books sitting on top looking as if he had recently used them. Only one, "Reward: Anthology of Unsolved Crimes of the Last Three Decades," had a post-it note marking a page.

I looked it up at the library's website and put it on hold. I had to swing by and check it out so I could scan it later. It was such a long shot and might be a waste of time.

I then glanced over the files of Gloria and Vincent Vanders and Donald Guy. I was looking for clues of how I could get gossip on them, or something. I had to stop before I had a solid plan. It was time for me to walk across the lake via the walkway and foot bridge for the wedding rehearsal. It was just as important for me to be in attendance since they may have special requests and needs they hadn't previously realized.

I locked up all the files, grabbed my work notebook and phone, and locked up my office. I hoped to have a plan of action for my evening by the time the rehearsal ended.

I had never attended or heard about Indian weddings, so the mixing of Indian traditions with American surprised me. They ran through the planned speech the minister would give explaining the bride wearing a red and white sari for prosperity and fertility and how the brightly colored saris for the bridesmaids were traditional. He explained how the henna on the bride and her attendants symbolize joy, beauty, spiritual awakening, and offering. Ariya and her bridesmaids already displayed some elaborate henna tattoos on their hands. There were eight bridesmaids and only three groomsmen including Liam, which was another of the many surprises this wedding held.

It was clear that Ariya wasn't attempting to incorporate Hindu traditions in an American wedding, but honor her heritage as part of who she is in the joining of two people. It was touching how they had melded recognition of both heritages. I briefly let my mind wonder if Mason had any thoughts on marriage ceremonies, then mentally slapped myself upside my head.

Liam regularly made eye contact as if he were checking up on me. I was busy making notes of things I noticed to make the event run smoothly. But I caught most of the rehearsal.

At the beginning an Indian man took the raised dais and explained he would do the traditional Ganesha Puja, a Hindu prayer to Lord Ganesh for good luck to be granted to the married couple and any obstacles they may encounter be destroyed.

Ariya approached me at the end of the rehearsal and I ran over the highlights of what I would do before the wedding tomorrow for her.

"You've thought of items I wouldn't have considered. Thank you." She bowed her head with a composure I never heard of in a bride. "In the Hindu wedding tradition we celebrate for three days, I've changed that to tonight's rehearsal dinner starting the celebration, then tomorrow the reception after the wedding continuing it, and the day after the wedding my father-in-law has offered to host a party at his home that would be the Indian traditional reception equivalent given by the groom's family. I would like to extend you an invitation to all events." She handed me a colorful hand lettered invitation.

"Thank you Ariya, I'm honored and touched. I'll try to attend at least one. Unfortunately, tonight I'm not able to join the rehearsal dinner." I knew it was a breach of the rules, but the day after the wedding they would no longer be clients so I might drop in for a few minutes.

I couldn't take too much time away from my finding answers about the murder victim's connection to myself and the resort.

"Liam said you would clear our bringing flowers for the rehearsal dinner. I hope that wasn't a problem." Ariya smiled.

"No problem, and I also alerted the restaurant to have diabetic dessert options for your mother-in-law. Will she require anything else?" I seemed to have completed my duties.

The group filtered out and over to the Clasico Italiano for the rehearsal dinner. Liam walked with me.

"I can't stay, I simply wanted to ensure there are no glitches." I explained. I was anxious to go.

"I wanted to explain, Ariya was raised far more Hindu than I. She shared that aspect with our mother more than I did." He seemed concerned about my perception.

"I'm not sure why you're telling me this. The rehearsal made it sound lovely."

"I just think you should know in case that conflicts with your beliefs."

"We aren't dating, you understand that, right?" I was growing a tad concerned what he thought our status was.

"I know, but in case that might weigh into your giving me chance. I just wanted to be up front." I wasn't sure what to think and Liam was soon pulled away by the wedding party to my relief.

Everything was set for the dinner, they had lovely centerpieces with big yellow flowers in several centerpieces down the length of the table and nothing left for me to supervise. It was time for me to go to a topless bar. I never thought I would ever say that!

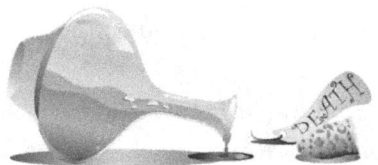

CHAPTER 14

*I*n the file on Donald Guy it said Rogers usually found him at a strip club. Fortunately, the file listed which one because there were several that PI Rogers visited in his quest for Mr. Guy of the insurance fraud infamy.

I decided my business clothes would suffice because if I went home I would chicken out. So my reserved suit in grey with a blush silk blouse was it.

But before I took the plunge at the "gentleman's club" I stopped by Donald Guy's apartment complex that was less than a mile from his favorite haunt.

It wasn't a luxury place, but it wasn't a slum either. It comprised one large apartment building of tan brick with small balconies for each unit, and barely a strip of grass in the front of the building along the street. It had one entrance to access the separate units, which I always thought was better for security. The grounds were clean and the surrounding neighborhood was primarily older but well maintained homes.

I hadn't prepared what I was doing or how I would approach anything. I got out of my car and leaned against it. Should I go inside? Doubtful I could learn anything staring at his door.

I had been debating what to do for only a minute or two when a middle-aged woman approached, car keys in hand.

"If you're looking to rent, I can show you the only unit I have available tomorrow." She said with a professional smile.

Wow, just that easily a way to proceed was handed to me. "I don't know. A girlfriend lives here, but she has complained about one neighbor, Donald somebody. Have you gotten many complaints about him or is it just my friend doesn't like him?" I held my breath when she stopped walking and scrutinized me.

"That particular resident has been asked to move. I don't put up with the likes of him. I assure you he won't be here in two weeks and I've already let the apartment association know of him so he won't get into a reputable place." She ground out.

"I hope it wasn't just a simple misunderstanding. I mean, I believe in following rules but a slight whoops surely wouldn't result in being thrown out." I put on my innocent female act, which contrary to popular belief I thought I pulled off quite well.

"Dear, this is a man to steer clear of. He thinks rules don't apply to him, he's argumentative, confrontational, and talk about anger management issues. I promise you, the rest of the residents are quiet and get along well for a pleasant community." She handed me her card.

I made some vague promises of stopping by tomorrow and she drove off.

I hadn't moved from leaning against my car door when a woman yelled from a third-floor window, "Don't move, I'm coming down." I looked around, seemed she was talking to me.

A twenty something young lady came trotting over in a minute, "I heard you talking to the landlady. Really this is a nice little place, and once Donald the Menace has moved out, it will be even better. We need more nice gals here, anyway." She smiled in her attempt to persuade me.

"Is this guy really all that bad? It seems hard to believe."

"He hasn't been here but maybe five months and, you know, I have nothing against smoking weed, but this guy thinks everybody should tolerate the cloud of smoke coming out of his door. Then, when he ain't high – which at least he's mellow then – he stomps around wearing a gun. I have nothing against open carry, I guess, but he uses his guns to intimidate anybody who looks at him funny. This place will be lovely when he finally moves out. I would love to have you for a neighbor." She had no clue that her sales pitch had done more to turn away a potential renter than encourage one.

This would sound silly, I knew it before I opened my mouth, "Really a gun you say. So, you don't worry he would use poison on the landlady or neighbors who've complained? You know, something sneaky and harder to prove." Pathetic, I know.

She looked at me like I hadn't been listening, "No he's definitely a shoot you then beat the body with the gun type of guy." She walked back inside shaking her head like I was simple-minded.

That was probably all I would get here, time for my next stop.

I had no idea what I was in for. I wasn't even clear if you called them strip clubs or topless bars. But, I knew I would have a difficult time getting any information. Somehow I had to make it work.

The Naughty Recess looked more like an industrial building on the outside with black corrugated siding. I parked close to the door so I could make a fast exit. Relief shot through me when I spotted a "no guns and weapons" sign at the entrance, so I wouldn't have to worry about Donald the Menace shooting the place up. I took a few moments for a self pep talk. I could do this, the sooner I found something out the sooner I could leave and try to forget this night. *How did I get into these situations, first serving court orders and now this?*

I got in free because female guests were such a novelty… unless they swung that way. Which, I definitely didn't. It was a typical bar, subdued lighting, plenty of neon signs, music, and a bar, except for the topless waitresses and dancers at poles and onstage barely wearing a g-string. This was nothing like a women's locker room, no matter how much I tried to tell myself it was no different. *What had I been thinking?*

I opted to down a drink… or two. The topless gal tending bar probably worked days at Hooters with her assets. But she took pity on me.

"You look uncomfortable. Waiting for your husband?" She smiled in sympathy. I liked her immediately. She wore a dog collar with her name, Chantilly, velcroed on.

Note to self: ask any man I'm serious about if they visit such *gentlemen's clubs*, because I didn't have a high opinion of men who frequented such places based on the specimens present displaying behavior I considered the worst characteristics of the species.

"No, I'm hoping to pick up some gossip. But first," I froze wondering what I should order, my usual Mojito or Margarita or should I opt for the hard stuff, "um... I don't know what I want to drink."

Chantilly chuckled, "Well, I can give you a special on a shot of Scotch."

Scotch it was, and I downed it quickly for liquid courage. It burned and my throat closed; I gasped for air. Chantilly smacked a small glass of water on the bar. Bless her. Once I could breathe again and had wiped the tears from my eyes, I tried my luck.

"Chantilly, can I ask you some questions?" My voice was shaky, but I didn't want to take the time for it to recover.

"If you're with a newspaper or doing a sociology report on strippers or something, no you can't." Her mouth set in a frown.

"Oh, no. Nothing like that. I, ummm, work for a private investigator who recently died and I'm going through his cases to finish them." Where had that come from? It jumped out all on its own without my brain engaging at all. I waited to see if she would accept it.

"Yeah, I heard Ricky died. He was a regular lately, didn't tip worth crap." Her face relaxed again. "Be right back." She had a customer down the bar ordering drinks. I swear she did a little jiggle of her assets and got rewarded with cash slipped in her collar. Oh, shoot me, please.

She returned, no jiggle for me. "So, what case brings you here that you want information on?"

"It involves a Donald Guy, that's the name. His notes said he frequents here." Which already told me a good bit about him as far as I was concerned.

Chantilly pointed to a skinny pale guy with a hawk nose, aviator styled prescription glasses, and short but kinky brown hair. He wore a tan western shirt and boot cut jeans to go with his silver tipped cowboy boots. He was watching a pole dancer, practically drooling and licked his lips as if the woman was a steak and he was starving. I just might be physically ill.

In the file, Rick Rogers had written days and times the guy had worked on some under the table roofing jobs when he was collecting disability payments. But no photos, which seemed a good motive for murder.

Insurance fraud was jail time and fines. Not huge, but my research said twenty-five thousand dollar fines and six months in jail. That's if it was a private insurance, if it was Social Security disability fraud I understood it was hundreds of thousands in fines and years in prison since that was a felony.

Yep, he had plenty of motive for murder.

Watching him, I swear I felt my skin literally crawl. But I didn't recognize him from any of the security videos, but there had been a few walking around in cowboy boots that seemed out of place to me at the time.

"I know, he gives the creep vibe all right."

"Did Ricky and Donald talk much?"

"Yeah, I wouldn't say they were good pals, but they partied here together, got private lap dances and stuff together. The girls said they were both sleazy and had to keep them from breaking the rules."

"Rules?"

"We may be topless, but turning tricks is still illegal so there are certain lines that can't be crossed even in the private rooms."

"Did they ever argue?" I couldn't imagine sleazy Donald would take blackmail easily. He gave off the feeling that he had a screaming fast and explosive anger and his neighbor thought he would shoot first and ask questions later.

"That's why I wouldn't call them close friends. They got into an argument a few months back and after that they only sat together a few times, the joint lap dances stopped. Then last week creepy Donald yelled about how he couldn't afford to keep paying and punched Ricky in the gut. They were tossed out and Donald has just been allowed back." She looked at me expectantly and I realized she was talking so easily because she expected an excellent tip.

"Anybody else have a problem with Ricky?" I was just fishing now.

She had another customer wander up to the bar to order, no doubt to get the jiggle treatment.

Before she returned a man tapped me on the shoulder. "If you're looking for work, we can take an application." He scrutinized me from head to toe and I felt more invaded than any airport security scan.

"No, no, no. I'm not here for work. I have a good job. Thanks." This couldn't be happening to me.

He screwed his mouth up like he was evaluating or doing math and it wasn't easy for him. "I bet I can top your wages. How does four hundred a night sound? If you'll do a naughty secretary strip on stage, you're tips could bring in more." He waggled his eyebrows like Groucho Marx.

I was speechless. Sure that was decent money, but not enough for the ogling and objectifying, or the pawing I noticed the gals slapped away.

"No. I'm not interested. Ever."

He looked me up and down again, "Shame, we could use you here. You might bring in a better class of guys." He wondered off.

Chantilly finally returned with more cash in her collar, "I see the boss is interested in you. Thinking of joining us here?"

I fished out a tip and my business card, "Even better. If you want to get a job where you're not treated like a slab of meat, don't have to jiggle like jello, and be fully clothed, call me."

She at least looked it over. "Naw, this is good work." But she tucked my card in her dog collar along with the cash tip.

I got home and showered, soaping up twice. I still felt grungy.

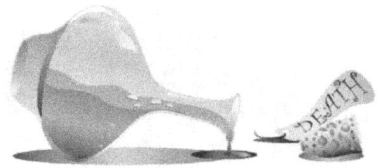

CHAPTER 15

There was a note slipped under my office door when I arrived at work early the next morning.

Stop asking questions. Curiosity killed the cat was printed in large type on standard printer paper.

Oh joy, after a hideous evening last night in a dive "gentleman's" club I now got threats. Perfect. At least it probably wasn't Donald the Menace who was more likely to have walked in with a gun to intimidate me than the no confrontation threatening note.

This wasn't my first threatening note in my life either. My first was last fall, and I found it on my bed at home. So this note slipped under my office door wasn't as unsettling by far.

I grabbed a saved grocery bag and slipped it inside. I would keep it for Detective Lawrence if he wanted to grill me again.

This brought to my mind the newspaper article yesterday with the barely veiled suspicions about my association with another murder.

I wanted to stop, especially after the seedy club last night. But I couldn't let such suspicions go unanswered. I dug my cell phone from my purse and called Mr. Chalmers, esquire. He was the lawyer my father had hired last fall when I was under police scrutiny.

I was connected as soon as the receptionist heard my name. "Miss LaMere, your uncle informed me you might call me. How can I be of service? Surely no more dead bodies."

"Well, about that…" I told him about the newspaper article and how it cast suspicion on me simply because my card was found in Rogers' possession. "And can we keep this from my dad? I'll pay you myself."

"Maybe I should be on retainer if this will be a recurring problem?"

If I didn't know he lacked any sense of humor, I'd think that was a joke. Then I told him about the note. He crisply declared he was coming right over to collect it and take it to the police.

I got absorbed in some actual work but was soon interrupted by a knock on the door. I fully expected Mr. Chalmers, but I found Liam leaning on my door frame. He wore jeans again and a polo shirt.

I looked at him differently, really looked at him. Sure he was handsome but I think what really accentuated his looks was his seeming ease. How he lounged against the door with such confidence, appearing to be relaxed and not posing. He had a grace of movement that was masculine and typified that assurance.

"How long have you been there?"

A pleasant smile blossomed that told me he was

enjoying himself, "Just a few minutes. Long enough to see you bite your lip when you concentrate."

Even though he was a few feet away I felt like he was much closer. For a moment I wanted him close. I wanted to find out what Porsche had been telling me for years to not over think every relationship and just get swept away in the moment.

Then a voice joined us from around the corner of my door, "Excuse me."

What impeccable timing Mr. Chalmers possessed. I was grateful he interrupted the moment but didn't really want Liam to know about the note. Liam stepped aside, and I waved him in.

"Here it is, I put it in this." I handed the bag to him.

He sat his briefcase down, opened it, and withdrew two evidence bags large enough to hold letter sized items. He carefully withdrew the note with tweezers and placed it in an evidence bag, then took the bag I had it in and placed that in an evidence bag. Finally he fingerprinted me. Right there, in my own office.

"The forensic people must eliminate your prints from the note to see if the author left any." He explained.

Liam transformed from easy grace to taut and focused. He managed the note over Mr. Chalmers' shoulder and then made eye contact with me. This was exactly what I hoped to avoid. Great, just fantastic, his alpha male protective instincts would kick in now.

Mr. Chalmers left with a promise to call me with any developments. He wasn't out the door before Liam was by my side, taking me in his arms. I was grateful for the comfort. I hadn't realized how much I needed to borrow a little strength from such solace. At least I didn't cry, or give into my earlier impulse to live in the moment.

"What have you been up to?"

"I take offense at that." But I retraced my steps over the last few days. I'd been busy between the wedding preparations, meeting Rogers competitor Mike Hammond, and the bar last night. I initially wasn't going to share about the topless bar, but it came out anyway. I didn't think volatile Donald Guy had seen or noticed me, but the bartender could have said something to him and I had given her my business card.

"This has gotten out of hand, love. You need to be safe and drop this." His voice was measured and calm.

Sure, it sounded reasonable. It was reasonable, so it was completely unreasonable for me to want to push back and tell him he didn't own me.

I shook my head yes even though inside I was resisting.

"I'll back off, okay?" I didn't say what that meant. I would try to not ask any outright questions like I had been. I would revert to gossip and research. The tried-and-true method.

"Then let's have lunch together. I haven't much longer before I fly back and I'd like to spend as much time with you as possible."

"I have…" He interrupted my thought with a kiss. A tender kiss on the lips with a hint of passion lurking that only lasted a few seconds.

I looked into his eyes and knew I could fall for him, but there was a part of me that held back. I wasn't sure if it was because I still held some abandonment issues left from my mother combined with his living in London or if I was holding out for Mason. Mason might be a moot point and I wasn't sure waiting for him wasn't avoidance too.

I placed a hand on his face, a caress. "I would love to, but I actually have a luncheon I'm attending."

His eyes searched mine. I wasn't sure what he was looking for.

"Okay. But I'll see you at the wedding this evening, right?" His voice was hopeful and compelling.

I nodded.

I was on remote control the rest of the morning, taking care of email and phone calls, directing items and details. But I felt up in the air. I needed to get things resolved, both for Roderick Rogers and for myself.

I knew Gloria Vanders was on the tape, so she had been around the Resort when Rogers was poking around, and the Sheriff and Commissioner, but what about Mike Hammond and Donald Guy? I could print out a photo of Hammond from the reality show website, and I had a snapshot I took of Donald Guy last night that would work, even though it was low lightning, that I could show around a few of the restaurants and security folks. I didn't have time to scan through the hours and hours of video again. I printed out a photo of Vincent Vanders while I was at it.

I printed the photos all on one sheet of paper and targeted the most likely restaurants. I wish I would've done this sooner, because the employees tried but saw so many faces each day. Several felt they had seen Hammond, but then I found out they watched Real

Investigators reality show. I stopped by the security office and showed Ron, the manager, and a few others coming and going the photos. No luck there either.

I gave up showing the photos around. I had to get on the road for the luncheon, anyway. I rushed to my office, grabbed my purse, and took off toward the parking at a fast walk.

I got to the luncheon downtown a little early and parked in the hotel's underground parking structure. There were only two classy hotels downtown and this was the older of the two. It wasn't luxury on the level of my resort, but it was nice and perfect for charity luncheons.

Dr. Gloria Vanders was a sponsor for the event helping to cover some of the costs, so I assumed she would attend. This was to benefit a local abused women's shelter. As attendees filtered into the large luncheon room, I was relieved to see several people I knew from the resort that I had either coordinated events for or was their liaison as resort members.

I found my table in the middle of the main ballroom. It was carpeted in a plush pile and the soft golden wallpaper with white trim gave the room a glow. There were several modern chandeliers with drapes of crystals giving soft lighting. There were about thirty large round tables with golden tablecloths and white fabric napkins set for eight people per table.

Linda Daryn, the wife of a retired lawyer, approached me and we hugged briefly. She had short light brown hair in an angled bob cut that accentuated her heart-shaped face and she wore an elegant yellow spring dress that made her look chic.

"I'm so glad to see you here. It's about time we get you involved more with the community." She bowed her head closer, "That mention of you in the paper was beyond the pale."

"Thank you, I appreciate that." I wasn't sure what was appropriate to say. Should I mention I got a lawyer or that it seems like Tiffany has a vendetta? My mother used to say when in doubt about what to say, keep your mouth shut. So I did just that.

But I was here to get gossip, so I had to say something.

"I expect I'll recognize a few people as resort clients. Like Dr. Vanders and her husband." Okay, I opened the door.

"She'll be here, no doubt. But that husband of hers is probably out…" She stopped and looked at me, "Have you met Vincent Vanders? Please tell me you aren't one of his conquests?"

Wow, back it up. That was a fast leap to a conclusion. Had Vincent been making the rounds a lot and everyone knew – making it the worst kept secret?

"I've never met the man, actually. But it sounds as though I don't want to either. But, he can't really be that bad. Surely Dr. Vanders would've divorced him if that were the case." Rolling out the red carpet for her.

"Oh, let me tell you. He's appalling. I hear he seduced a teen daughter of one of Gloria's close friends, in Gloria's house. I don't know who the girl might be, but he's scandalous."

She paused long enough to scan the room, then continued in a lower voice as if this was even worse. "She can't divorce him until she proves his indiscretions or he'll get half her net worth and property." She gave me a meaningful look which I interpreted as considerable money at stake.

Now to lead her by the hand. "That should be a simple matter of hiring a private investigator, I would think." I tried to display a concerned but helpful look.

"Well, I don't know what happened there. I thought she had hired someone but low and behold she hasn't left the… the… moron." She struggled to find a word. A few came to my mind but she probably wouldn't appreciate the low-brow sleazy man-whore I would use. I know, my bad.

Linda Daryn suddenly waved to a lady across the room and dashed away. I looked around for anybody else I might know, only to have my Aunt Regina and cousin Felicia tap me on the shoulder. Auntie was dressed up in a silky lavender dress and matching pumps. Felicia wore a muted rose pink flowing dress with lace accents and a few tasteful ruffles, the epitome of feminine as usual.

Felicia gave me a hug, and I was enveloped in her light citrusy perfume. This was her way of trying to make up for not keeping my investigation from her parents. I whispered in her ear, "You don't get off that easy. You've a lot of kissing up to do." That gave me an idea.

"We're over at the far table, if I knew you were coming we could've gotten assigned to sit together." Aunt Regina fussed.

"I had no idea you two were involved in this organization or in community fundraising." Which was true, they had surprised me.

"I'm stealing Felicia away for a moment." I linked arms with my cousin and dragged her into the brightly lit reception and registration area and away from the crowd.

"I need you to gather gossip for me. Dr. Vanders is a sponsor and she'll probably be here. Can you try to find out if she or her husband have bad tempers or are vindictive?"

"I don't know Julie." There was a distinct whine in her tone.

"You owe me big for your blabber mouth. Time to pay up." I was older by two years and we had grown up like sisters, so I considered this within my sisterly realm to push and coerce. Isn't that what big brothers and sisters do?

"If you find out where they were four days ago in the early morning too, that would be really helpful. You know, were they anywhere near the resort then?"

She narrowed her eyes. "You're bullying me into helping with that PI's death."

"It's only for this luncheon. That's just a matter of minutes here and there as you're eating and chatting with folks, anyway. I know you can do it."

"Then you'll forgive and forget my letting it slip the other day?" She was shrewd, she wanted confirmation. She would do fine getting information.

I nodded. "Whatever you do, don't tell your folks."

She stuck her tongue out at me. Two years may not seem like a big difference, but at the moment she seemed so juvenile. Sadly, I wanted to stick mine out at her in return. Family has a way of doing that to us, am I right?

We returned to the ballroom and the noise level had

already grown as more people got seated. I weaved through the growing crowd to my assigned table and I was surprised to find Elaine Burke, a friend of Linda Daryn, and her golfer husband seated at my table.

"Mrs. Burke, so nice to see you again. I saw Linda just a moment ago." I hoped I didn't come across too familiar.

She stood and came around the table to give me a hug. I guess familiar was okay in this setting.

In a stage whisper she joked, "I'm glad to have somebody to talk to dear, Jack is so dull at these things." Sure enough, Jack sat like a zombie and stared ahead, nothing like when he was golfing with his buddies at the resort.

"This is my first time, so I'd appreciate your showing me the ropes." That's my way of setting up a reason for the curiosity I was about to show.

She winked. "I understand dear. It really is all about who you know. Fortunately, you're acquainted with a few folks through the Resort. I can introduce you to a few well-connected folks too."

I wondered why she would be so willing to introduce me around. What did she think I was here for? Drumming up business for the resort, maybe?

"Somebody mentioned Gloria Vanders. Who is she?" I started slow with Elaine.

"Well, she's a fixture at these functions and the Country Club set. She's a well known Oncologist from a society family back east." She cocked her head and narrowed her eyes.

"She sounds like an interesting person." I toned it down, I might have tipped my hand.

"Just stay away from her husband. He hasn't any

money, and he uses women then tosses them aside. I don't care if he sweet talks you, don't go near him." She gave me a stern look.

"Oh, no. I wouldn't… he's married after all." I stuttered. Way to go LaMere, she thinks you're interested in Vincent.

"Take my advice and stay far away from the Vanders. They're both vindictive if they don't get their way. I don't want to lose my favorite Resort contact." Good to know I was a favorite. *They were both vindictive huh?*

"I'm surprised to hear that about a lady of such… upbringing." I tried for a mildly scandalized look.

"It happens, even in good families. Tragic." She shook her head gently.

"Well, sounds as if the scoundrel husband causes her bad temper if he's so loose."

She considered that for a few seconds, "He certainly hasn't helped her disposition, but she was like that before him. I can't in good conscious lay the blame solely at his feet. And he, well, he's nearly a thug. I think she was swayed by a bad boy who doesn't want to change."

"Does a leopard ever change his spots?" I was thinking of Mason at the moment and his single-guy mentality.

"From what I've observed, no, they do not." She shook her head no. "Better to find a good solid, dependable man you can count on, like my Jack."

I didn't know Maytag built that line of product. I glanced at Jack sitting and starring into the distance and wondered if that was really better. There must be dependable men who were engaged in their wife's interests, weren't there? Please don't burst my bubble.

"Surely her husband isn't as bad as a common thug?" I was going for the golden ring now.

"I remember when she married him, there was a rumor that surfaced. Claimed Vincent had put a man in the hospital for double crossing him on a real estate deal. Now, I don't like repeating such things but I wonder if there might have been some truth to it since the rest of his character is so lacking."

The luncheon was starting as a woman stood at the podium in front and tapped a spoon against a water glass for attention.

I had plenty to think about while I ate. Vincent Vanders or his society wife Dr. Vanders seemed prime suspects. I wonder how I could find out more about Vincent's whereabouts. But I felt I had forgotten something important.

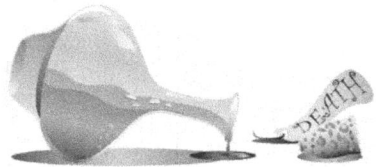

CHAPTER 16

The food portion of the luncheon was done, and I'd sat through a few testimonials about all the good work the charity did. I had even written a check and placed it in an envelope for the table captain to collect. I was antsy to get going since it seemed my opportunity for chatting and gossip was over, when I noticed Felicia get up, look my way, and walk to the lobby doors. I followed after her with a slight speed walk to catch her, but I needn't have tried so hard.

She was waiting for me in the lobby. She grabbed my hand and led me to a quiet corner.

"I wanted to tell you what I found without mom asking a bunch of questions. A friend of Dr. Vanders' was our table captain. She sure had no trouble sharing what a miscreant hubby Vincent is." She was excited, talking in a conspiratorial whisper.

Not much new there, Vincent seemed to be the favorite topic for gossip. No wonder Gloria wanted rid of him, no woman wants to be the topic of the society luminaries' gossip. As a Doctor Gloria would know all about poisons and maybe Vincent used her references or resources to look for a poison. Because of her job either one of them might have had easy access to poisons. Linda had mentioned he was vindictive, or was it Elaine?

"I found out that Vincent plays tennis at your Resort nearly every day. Some say he hangs out there to pick up lonely rich women or their daughters. He sounds like such a dog. I think you might catch him there today even. Just be careful, they say women can't resist him." Her eyebrows crinkled together.

I laughed, "You're worried about me? Vincent can't possibly be more handsome or suave than Mason or Liam."

"Liam? That's the secret agent man, huh? You neglected to say how hot he was at dinner the other night."

I glared in reply, one of those looks my aunt was always leveling that causes an instant desire for the earth to swallow you. I didn't linger, but left after talking with Felicia.

I stopped by the library to pick up a copy of the book PI Rogers had in his office after the luncheon. It had been in the photo I took of Rogers' office and had a post-it note marking a page. I wanted to scan through the book to see if there was anything of relevance.

Next, I made a stop at home. I had to work late because of the wedding starting at five and I should be present to handle any issues that arise. So I was taking time now to get some snooping done.

I was hoping to meet my Resort Irregulars at the

mailbox, so I made a beeline there after parking. I opened my mailbox and stood for a while looking through my mail. Just as I was walking away, Delores hailed me.

"Hey lady, wait up." She didn't hurry though.

"Any news for me?" I still wanted to get back to work. If nothing else I could go through the library book.

"No pleasantries? I'm okay, thank you. Arthritis is flaring up in my hands but I took some of that Glucosamine over-the-counter stuff. But, don't worry about me any dear."

"I'm sorry to have been rude. Just trying to get back to work and wanted to see if you had anything for me." I didn't mean to hurt her feelings.

"Sure, just use me and toss me aside. Like a man, get everything you want from me and then don't call or even get together for coffee." She cocked her hip and planted a hand on it.

"Um, sorry?" I didn't think I wanted to know what she was talking about. She rolled her eyes.

"I talked to my Bunco game pals and one lady's husband works in the Sheriff's department. Everyone there knows about the affair, but it isn't widely known outside the department nor talked about openly. Her husband thinks it's been developing over the years and now is more... regular, I guess you would say." Her face looked like she ate a rotten pistachio.

Interesting, so it's not entirely a secret. But, if it's gotten more regular one or both spouses could be suspicious.

"Good information Beverly. Any idea if Shannon or Leland is the type to get revenge?"

"Oh my yes, Sheriff is spiteful. A newspaper article was critical of the Sheriff during an emergency situation and he fumed for weeks and wanted to get even. My friend's husband said they didn't know if he went through with anything, but he wouldn't be surprised. Called him a loose canon."

Lovely, just want you want in a law enforcement officer. All I discovered was that Rogers had a knack for blackmail and was coercing payments from Donald Guy to keep quiet on his insurance fraud, Vincent Vanders to not turn over the evidence needed to divorce him and leave him without a penny, and perhaps tried to blackmail a volatile Sheriff about his extra-marital affair with an elected county official. That could be the big fish he mentioned to Mike Hammond. Talk about playing with fire.

But poison was supposedly a woman's weapon of choice. The women involved were Gloria Vanders and Shannon Gage. Neither of them was involved with the resort other than a visit or stay, and I hadn't personally known them before to explain why Rogers would have my card.

Any of them could have also killed Peggy Faire if she tried to take over the blackmail enterprise. But how do you poison a person who is likely wary of you because her boss was killed that way? I doubted Peggy would take a drink from one of the blackmail victims. But then I didn't know how the killer had poisoned Rogers while at the resort. Wonder if Liam could get that information from the police somehow.

I felt like I was on a merry-go-round and kept coming

back to the beginning. I snapped my fingers, remembering what had been at the edges of my thoughts, Rogers had asked about Mr. Marks or something sounding like that, which didn't seem connected to any of these suspects. I made a mental note to follow up on the mysterious Mr. Marks.

I came back to the moment with Delores. "If this has been going on a long time, I wonder why one of their spouses chose now to get an investigator. Did your friend say anything had changed recently for Leland or Shannon?" I was thinking out loud more than anything.

If I had the missing file on the cheating couple, so many of these questions might be answered.

"No, nothing like that was mentioned."

"Thanks Delores, I have to get back to work. I appreciate your finding that out." I turned to leave, but Delores placed her hand on my arm.

"Be careful. I didn't like how they described the Sheriff, he's a nasty piece of work." Her eyes were overflowing with worry.

"I promise I will." With that I hustled back to my car and work.

I dropped my purse off in my office and scurried across the resort campus south over to the tennis club and its multiple courts. The courts were primarily for pro lessons and tennis drills, but there were some limited hours for members to use one court. I was betting from everything I had heard, Vincent Vanders would hang around the club preying on women even if he didn't play a set.

The resort's tennis club had made it into the top

twenty tennis resorts again this year. We had a stellar pro staff for lessons and drills and the setting was phenomenal. Evergreen and aspen trees were sprinkled around the courts perfuming the air with pine scent and the music of leaves fluttering. To the west you could look across the velvety green golf links and see majestic Pikes Peak glimmering in the afternoon sun, still snow capped at just over fourteen thousand feet.

I wasn't around the tennis club often, so I sought Robert who I had dealt with in the past. I found him inside at the sign-up desk.

Robert was tan, lean, and his head was topped with short spiked sandy brown hair. He was one of only two non-pro employees for the tennis club, handling the schedules and all administrative duties. The other club exclusive employee handled the smoothie bar on the other end of the club's main room with bistro tables and chairs scattered around.

Outside were several larger round tables with stripped umbrellas where guests sipped their smoothies or brought an alcoholic drink over from the bar at the nearby bistro.

The *thwacks* of rackets hitting balls serenaded us as two courts were busy running drills, the instructors voices muted as they gave pointers.

"What brings you round lady? Not that seeing you isn't the bright spot to my day, but it's rare to see you over here." He was charming in a laid back style, which was a hit with the tennis crowd.

I lowered my voice to avoid being overheard, "Vincent Vanders. Does he hang around the club?"

"Yes, he hangs around. Sometimes he even gets a

lesson, but usually he's trolling for women who aren't bothered by his occupied ring finger. Have some husbands been complaining?" Robert's smile turned to a scowl.

"Do you recall if he was around this last week or so?"

Robert stuck a lip out in thought, "Seems he has been around every few days for the last couple of weeks. I couldn't say which days though. Why?"

I had printed out a photo of the deceased Mr. Rogers and brought it with me, "Was this man around much or maybe spoke to Vanders?" I held my breath in anticipation.

He smiled, "You're on the money. Yes, that guy was around a good bit a few months back. I finally noticed he followed Vanders at a distance. But last week they got into an argument at one of the tables right out there." He motioned to the outdoor circular tables under umbrellas.

"How about a few days ago? Did you see Vanders or this guy around more recently?" I started to bite on my lip, but I remember my mother always stopping me. I began lightly tapping my foot instead.

Robert thought for several moments then nodded, "Sure, I remember Vanders seemed to leave one of the married guests abruptly and then I saw this guy," he tapped the photo, "trying to follow him. I hope that helps."

"You've been very helpful, thanks Robert."

"Speak of the devil." Robert pointed with his chin to the outdoor tables.

Vince Vanders sat down with a cocktail in one hand and an expensive sports bag in the other. He tossed the bag in a vacant chair and glanced at his Rolex. He brushed the chair off before sitting down. Guess he didn't want to get a speck of anything on his designer tennis outfit.

"Robert, does he have a lesson or drills?" I asked without breaking my examination of the philandering snake.

"No, he likes to appear like he is here for a legitimate reason when he's only trolling for wealthy married women." Robert's voice was like acid dripping.

"Can you tell me the last five women who have been his willing playmates please? Don't worry, it's only to confront him, I don't plan on ruining any marriages." They didn't need any help with that.

Robert told me, with a smile.

I walked outside and past his table with more sway and slower than my usual. He did not let me down. He whistled. I stopped and pivoted, slowly.

"I haven't seen you around before lovely lady." Despite his sunglasses I could feel his eyes and their invasive scan of my body.

"It's about time that changed, don't you think?" I growled.

He should have paid attention to my voice rather than my chest. If he had, he would have seen trouble coming.

"I couldn't agree more. I want to know all your favorite things… to do." His voice was low and suggestive.

Did women actually fall for this? I couldn't help comparing him to Liam, or even Mason. He came out severely lacking in style, class, and just panache. How could such a sleazy guy pick up so many women?

I walked up and leaned over him, "I am the assistant manager of this resort."

"You must know all the vacant rooms."

"What I know is that Mrs. Courtland, Mrs. Warren, Mrs. Kirkson, Mrs. Talbert, and Mrs. Byrd are all guests here that you've been seducing. This isn't your personal pickup joint. I just left a fundraiser with your wife, I'm sure she'd love to know all about your married conquests so she can contact their husbands, or just call her lawyer."

His dark golden tan had turned a chalky gray and his Adam's apple was bobbing.

"If I hear of another incident of you playing Casanova with my guests, your wife is my first phone call." I leaned closer, "I'm watching you, and Gloria is on my speed dial." I stood up tall and looked down at him. "Whoever you're waiting for will have to be disappointed. You're leaving. Now." I crossed my arms.

He left his drink, grabbed his shiny sport bag, and trotted away. I glanced inside and Robert was clapping with a big smile on his face.

It was a few hours before the wedding so I first made the trek across the lake via the built up walk way that split the lake in two halves.

The wedding preparations were in full swing and the hall was a buzzing hive of activity. The florist had a team of helpers running around with flowers, fabric, and various accessories. The floral scents clung in the air heavy and cloying. I was expecting springtime colors for the flowers, but instead the dramatic blood red and pure white floral sprays and bouquets jarred the eyes.

I was relieved to see the arch was in place and the

florist had already draped it with a gauzy white fabric and a large red dahlia swag. Behind the archway were three large floor standing candelabras with eight red candles each waiting to be lit. The archway was flanked on each side by massive floral sprays and the same wispy white fabric swirled around the flower stands. Big white satin bows with bunches of red flowers were attached to each aisle seat. There was a red carpet down the aisle and the walls were draped with more white twinkle lights than I've ever seen in one place, lighting the scene in a soft glow.

It looked like a red and white romantic dream. I would have to remember this for any winter holiday weddings. I checked on Chef Claude and found him in full swing for the reception dinner.

The reception in the Grand Ballroom wasn't setup yet, that would probably begin after the wedding venue was finished. Everything was running smoothly and everyone had my number if they needed anything so I returned to my office until time for the wedding itself.

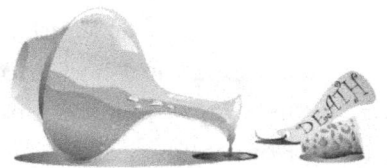

CHAPTER 17

*B*ack in my office I made notes from the luncheon and talking to Delores. The main suspects were primarily Sheriff Leland Morrison and County Commissioner Shannon Gage.

The sheriff was known to be spiteful and a loose cannon. I didn't know much about Shannon yet though. But the affair had built up over time, so either a spouse was just now figuring it out, or something changed to spur hiring Rogers.

I paced in a tight little circle to help myself think.

Shannon as a woman was more likely to use poison. Motive was to stop being blackmailed and to keep the affair from their spouses and the resulting public divorce that could lose them their jobs. They were staying at the hotel and thus could have slipped a poison to Rogers somehow. Although, slipping him some poison probably wouldn't be easy when he is following your every move and likely kept at a distance. Besides, I didn't know if they had access to whatever poison was used. But that would be the same issue with all the suspects.

I stood still for a bit.

My second prime choice, Dr. Gloria Vanders had a temper, was reportedly vindictive, and as a woman was more likely to use poison. Vincent Vanders was rumored to put a man in the hospital and had a lot of money to lose in a divorce. Gloria was on tape arguing with Rogers, so she definitely had opportunity if it was a slow acting poison that took a good day or so.

I was back to pacing in small circles.

Donald Guy was running an insurance disability scam that could land him in prison and was quick to anger too. Motive was to stop blackmail, but I didn't know about opportunity or access to any poison. Besides, poison took patience and subtly he didn't seem to possess.

I sat down but my foot was bouncing.

That left rival investigator Mike Hammond who was quick to say Rogers had lost interest in getting a regular spot on the reality show because he had a bigger fish to reel in. That fish could have meant the Sheriff. But I only had Hammond's word about his loss of interest in the competition and they had gotten into a fistfight after all. But slipping a person some poison was pre-meditated. Could the competition have gotten so dirty that Hammond snapped and planned to murder Rogers? That just seemed weak. Although, who really knew what could snap a person.

I noted Leland and Shannon's spouses too. I didn't think of the spouses as prime suspects. But, I could see a fit of anger over withholding proof that you paid Rogers to obtain and discovering his extorting money from your two-timing spouse to keep the evidence quiet might push a person over the edge.

I was drumming my fingers on the desktop.

Rogers may not have deserved to be murdered, but he sure had been asking for it when he tangled with so many dangerous people. Except for the Sheriff and Commissioner, the rest didn't really have much of a connection to the resort, and not with me.

There was always the possibility of a person I didn't know about, or a connection to Rogers I didn't know about. I thought that was a viable option in this maze of deception.

Then there was Rogers asking me about a Mr. Marks. I took a trip to the check-in desk yet again to access the reservations and past guests. One of these days they would give me access to that system from my office computer. The lobby was quiet at the moment with only a few people wandering in or out and meeting others before leaving.

I searched for Mr. Marks in the last two years of the records and came up with one guest, Jacob Marks, who had only stayed for two nights and that was around eighteen months ago and he was from New York. It was old news and I couldn't see how that would mean anything a year and a half later.

I returned to my little closet of an office and continued pondering the case.

This mystery man Mr. Marks could be the unknown element, a person I don't know about or his connection in this mess. I looked through the client files quickly again and there was no Mr. Marks mentioned anywhere, even tangentially to Mr. Rogers' cases. A Facebook search without the first name was useless; I got back hundreds of results for Colorado alone.

I still came back to the fact that there was no file on the Sheriff and Commissioner. In my mind that was nearly a smoking gun and would explain Peggy's death too. She might have been foolish enough to blackmail one or the other. They at least had a connection to the hotel for Rogers to have my business card.

It would be nice to know how long it took the poison to take effect, but I didn't have alibis or even whereabouts of my suspects so it was moot. I may not definitely clear the hotel or myself of a connection.

It was time for me to run to the other side of the lake for the wedding and focus on that part of my job. I was early enough to help with some last-minute items they hadn't thought of, like a power cord.

The introduction of the wedding explained the mixing of cultures and that red and white were traditional for blessing the couple. That explained the flower colors, and it made perfect sense now.

Ariya entered wearing a stunning red sari with Indian jewelry including a long jeweled piece that lay along the part of her hair with an elaborate pendant on the end resting on her forehead. She was exquisite. The groom was wearing a classic white tux with a red boutonniere.

Then the Hindu prayer to Lord Ganesh for the couple's good luck was given. The bride and groom exchanged long flower garlands which was their mutual agreement to the ceremony, which I found an interesting idea. They exchanged golden necklaces then did the standard western vows and ring exchange.

I thought it was beautiful with the mixing of cultures, and unique to the couple. I wasn't sure how the groom's father, Landon Garrett and wife Lillian felt since they were stone faced from the glimpses I got.

As I was surveying the audience and looking for anything I should address, I was amazed to see Sheriff Leland Morrison in attendance. He sat with his wife who I recognized from the photos I found online. I might have a chance to speak to them casually. I couldn't imagine him being friends of Ariya or Jason, but he could be a friend of Jason's parents.

I left before the end so I could check on progress of the reception setup. The centerpieces of silk red and white rose balls sitting atop crystal candlesticks with matching circlets at the base coordinated with the white table clothes and red napkins. The stage was setup with large sprays of silk flowers and dyed Ostrich plumes in the red and white theme around the piano and back wall. The piano itself had red and white flower garland draped around it.

The food was all set and filling the room with mouth-watering smells. Other than a few fine details for the musicians that were arriving, everything appeared to be well in hand. The piano player jumped in with pop tunes to allow the other musicians time to settle in.

It wasn't long before people trickled in and staked claims to tables and the noise level crept upward. I had intended to leave after guests were filling up the grand ballroom, but I stayed for information on the Sheriff.

The wedding party would be busy with photos for a while. This gave me a chance to walk around and perhaps glean some information. I was wearing my name tag, so it was obvious I worked for the resort. I watched Sheriff Leland Morrison escorted his wife to a table close to the wedding party table.

Why hadn't Liam mentioned the philandering Sheriff was invited and apparently known by the family? He and his mistress were my top suspects since he met two of the three criteria, motive and opportunity.

My face always gave away my emotions or thoughts and I must have looked confused because a thirty some-thing young man who had stopped to watch the sheriff nudged me.

"You aren't familiar with good old Leland Morrison there, are you?" He was out to impress me was my first thought.

He was direct and that might work in my favor.

"He looks a little familiar, but I can't place him." I was leaving the door wide open for him to be the more knowledgeable and explain it all. Men love that, am I right? "Does he frequent the resort? Maybe I've seen him around."

"That is the county Sheriff and his wife, Constance." He looked me over in a cursory glance, "What do you do here?"

"I helped coordinate the wedding and reception." He didn't need to know I was the Assistant General Manager in-training. "I didn't realize the wedding party knew such influential people." I widened my eyes a bit and assumed a slight tone of awe.

"Well, I believe it's actually the Groom's father Mr. Garrett who's friends with the Sheriff."

That explained why Liam didn't say anything, he probably didn't know. The next part wouldbe hard for me. I gave him a shy smile and glanced his way playing coy, "You must be somebody important." Yeah, I could barely stand it myself.

He actually stood taller. "Well, I wouldn't say that. But, I know several key movers and shakers in town."

"Do you know the Sheriff personally then? I just wondered what he's like, cranky dealing with all those criminals?" I gave him a look of what I hoped was innocence and awe. I even added twisting my hair. All I was missing was some bubble gum and I would have to slap myself upside the head.

"He's ummm, well I've heard he's difficult to work for, very demanding and not very understanding. But, in such a position of authority the responsibility must weigh heavily on his shoulders." He said with the tone of a wise man. Did he think the Sheriff could hear him because he sounded like he was afraid to say anything that could get back to the man himself.

He leaned over in a conspiratorial fashion, "I know he doesn't play well with other departments."

I raised my eyebrows, "In what way?"

"Well, such as with other emergency personnel like the fire chief or the Forest Service head." He shrugged a shoulder as if it was no big deal, "Alpha male posturing I guess."

"Boundaries must be maintained." I nodded as if that explained everything. He sounded more like a man who threw his weight around. He wouldn't be the type to take a blackmail attempt from Rogers well at all. But I doubted he would use poison over a more direct approach.

Thirty-something man nodded in agreement. "There are a lot of whispers that follow him, but it's bound to happen with a powerful man who doesn't take any crap."

"Sure. I bet they say he has a string of women or…" I waited to see if he took the bait.

"Or he plays favorites with his staff and such." He scoffed.

"What about his wife, she must be very… proud?" It was hard to say such a thing. If he were my husband, he would be out on his sorry derrière in a very public display preferably when reporters were around. *Just saying.*

"I'm sure she is, naturally. She holds a certain place in the community because of his position too." He added as if he was the font of sage knowledge.

I took that to mean she wouldn't be happy at all with his philandering and embarrassing her, but would she hire an investigator and risk anybody else knowing about his unfaithful heart? More to the point, would she kill Rogers and Peggy Faire?

I changed my tactic a little. "Wasn't there a private detective who died in a car accident? Do the police and those hired investigators all know each other? They coordinate I would imagine." I gave him the big dumb eyes.

"I don't know about that. I think there are some territorial issues; at least I would imagine there would be with amateurs running around. Besides, with Leland's reputation for *boundary* issues I would imagine the paid detective would be a point of contention."

He took a swig of his red wine, "How about a dance when the music gets geared up? Or maybe we can go out for a drink when you're done for the night?"

Mr. thirty-something wasn't my type at all. It seemed my type was the dangerous and good looking type. Agent one-oh-seven and Bond Jr. were similar enough to make it a type. I never realized it before. A year ago I would have told you average loyal guy was my type, but never secret agent man.

"I've got to get back to work now. Bye." I wiggled my fingers in farewell and I took off like a thoroughbred out of the gate.

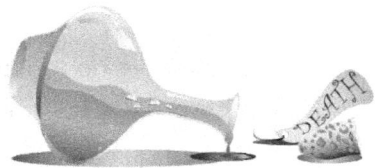

CHAPTER 18

I walked around the buffet table and noticed the Sheriff was deep in discussion with a woman and would probably be awhile. I removed my nametag then made a beeline over to the table where his wife Constance was sitting.

"Is this seat taken?"

"No, please join me. I hate sitting here by myself." She smiled and gestured to take a seat.

"Is there anything I can get you, ma'am? Maybe a drink?"

"That's kind, but no. My husband was getting me some wine." She had the air of a woman raised to be taken care of by a man.

I felt sorry for her, because sooner or later her world would come crashing down with a cheating husband like hers, unless she already knew. Images of the Sheriff on the security tape with his hands all over the Commissioner flashed in my mind.

"I'm Felicia." I figured my cousin still owed me for her big mouth.

"I'm Constance," she nodded her head to indicate Leland, "and that's my husband there talking to the blonde woman." She looked me over, scrutinizing. "Are you one of Leland's affairs checking out the wife?"

My face must have shown my alarm, or flat out shock. I hadn't expected that response. What kind of marriage makes a woman assume such a thing upon meeting another woman? My mouth hung open.

"I'm sorry, I didn't mean to shock you, but it's happened before. I find it easier to cut to the heart of the matter." Her expression was no-nonsense and defiant.

So, she was a fight-for-her-man sort of woman. Would she even bother to hire a detective? Then what about the Commissioner's husband? Did he hire Mr. Roger's.

"I most certainly am not, I assure you." I said with stiff formality and indignation. I wasn't going to share that I knew exactly who he was dallying with either. "You might want to hold back a bit more, what if I'd been a reporter?" I had to add that last part.

"I think his exploits are the best-known secret in town. If the paper hasn't done a story on his roving eye by now, they aren't interested." She let out a sigh.

That couldn't be easy to endure, everybody in town knowing your husband... dipped his wick with other women. I wanted to ask why she didn't drop-kick him to the curb, divorce him and make him pay for the humiliation. But her answer was probably more than I really wanted to know about their marriage. Maybe she was one of those women who will suffer anything to keep from divorcing.

"I know you must think me soft in the head to stay with a man who cheats. You young folk don't understand the commitment and sacrifices to keep a marriage together." She said with conviction as if I couldn't understand her trials.

Maybe if her tone hadn't been so superior I wouldn't have said anything, "Oh, I understand commitment and sacrifice, but what you have is a sham of a marriage or he would do some sacrificing rather than satisfying his lusts." Yeah, she got to me. I was thankful I had removed my nametag.

She pressed her lips together. I could believe her as the killer and if the daggers in her eyes she was shooting my way were any sign, she wouldn't lose any sleep over it either. But, she didn't seem like she would have hired Rogers in the first place. Even if Rogers' threatened he would go to the newspaper, it seemed doubtful the paper would bite if they hadn't done a story yet. That didn't mean that alpha male Leland wouldn't kill off a potential black-mailer. Shannon Gage was still a viable possibility though as she had plenty to lose personally.

A tap on my shoulder startled me and I looked up to see Liam in his white tux with red boutonnière and bowtie. He was intimidating all dressed up and looking so hot it should be illegal. He looked like a model for formal wear, he only had to pose like he was removing his tie. His brown eyes were glowing copper and his skin was radiant in the white suit that fit him so very well. He was wearing the exotic spicy cologne again. *Gulp*.

"Wedding photos all done?" I looked around and saw most of the wedding party was present. It seemed Landon and his wife weren't ready for the second act yet. I suspected the Hindu aspects of the ceremony were uncomfortable for them and they needed a moment to regroup.

"May I have a word, please?" He took my hand and smiled.

I glanced at Constance and she was already ignoring my existence. I was tempted, for a brief moment, to flaunt Liam angling for me rather than her reprobate husband, but it would be lost on her.

Liam and I stepped outside where dusk was fading into dark with only a few traces of the coral sunset left. The half moon was already rising.

"Did you see the Sheriff, he's actually a guest." His voice held a touch of surprise.

"I saw him and that was his wife I was chatting with." I gave him a smug smile. "It seems Landon Garrett and the Sheriff are acquaintances."

"Did you find out anything else?" He was close and his voice was low.

"The good sheriff's wife, Constance, knows all about his affairs, plural. She flat out asked if I was one."

For once I got a reaction from him as he shook his head in wonder.

I shared what little I found out from my luncheon about Gloria and Vincent Vanders, even my little encounter with Vincent. I hadn't shared my surveillance of Donald Guy and planned to keep that experience to myself. It would die with me.

"Is there any way you can find out from Detective Lawrence when Rogers was most likely poisoned and maybe what poison while you're at it?"

"I can call in the morning and give it a try."

"We've plenty of motives to spare, but we don't have a definite time of poisoning to try to develop a timeline and filter through any alibis." I let out a sigh.

"I love it when you talk to me like that." He leaned in and kissed me.

I blame the gentle breeze and half moon lighting the lake and the band playing a romantic song for the bride and groom's first dance.

It wasn't the sweet kiss from the other day; it was a full contact, take no prisoners, grabbing the brass ring kiss. It took me by surprise, but I responded and found electricity zinging from my toes to the top of my head.

I pulled away first, because as scintillating as it was, I imagined Mason kissing me. We both were breathing heavier. He rested his forehead against mine.

"Too fast, too soon?" His voice was husky and alluring with his accent.

I didn't know what to say. I couldn't tell him he gets an 'A' for technique and wow factor but hey, I wanted it to be somebody else. I couldn't tell him that, so I looked at the ground and said nothing.

"Oh. It's complicated, right? It's that bloke that saw us together, isn't it? You're really that over the moon for him even with whatever broke you guys up?"

I just nodded my head. If I had left right after the ceremony rather than hanging around playing detective I wouldn't have hurt Liam.

"I hope to have a woman like you so in love with me some day." He nudged my chin to look up at him. "I had to try, I couldn't let you be a memory without seeing if we could be more." He took a deep breath, "We'll talk tomorrow morning. Hopefully, I'll have something to report from the detective." He returned to the wedding reception with much less enthusiasm.

I stood and watched him walk away. Was I crazy to let him go? He was kind, a gentleman, had no problem with my career, intelligent, and leading-man Hollywood handsome. I sighed. Then I must be crazy. The heart wants what the heart wants and my heart wanted Mason. Or I wasn't over him yet and Liam deserved better than a rebound relationship.

I turned to walk back to my office and leave for the day. In the deepening dark I became hyperaware of how far I had to walk, alone. That note had been slipped under my office door only a few hours ago, not left for me at home, but here. My heart pounded against my rib cage. I couldn't ask Liam to escort me after the failed kiss.

I walked as though I were in a race, a speed walking race. I hesitated as I approached a section of sidewalk flanked by shrubs and trees that could hide a killer. As I hesitated for a brief second, I heard footsteps behind me. I stopped and listened; the footsteps stopped a few seconds after mine.

I was officially scared. I forced my feet to walk again, and I fumbled in my pockets for my phone. I wish I had my purse with my pepper spray. But it was in my office safe and secure.

I was closing in on the low walking bridge across the

manmade lake. My mind whirled. Anybody following me would risk being visible if they joined me on the bridge, but it would be easy enough to hit me over the head and dump me in the water since there were no rails on the wide built up walkway cutting through the small lake.

Anybody out or on the terrace across the way might not be looking this direction. It might be a chance somebody would risk. But I wasn't going to walk all the way around the lake to get to the main hotel where my office was.

I reached the walking path across the lake, the footsteps still behind me. I trotted onto the cement path edged with pebbles at a peppy but casual speed as if I weren't dog tired and was in a hurry. Every few steps I jogged.

I reached midway across the walkway and didn't hear any footsteps following. I risked a quick look behind, nobody was following me, but I thought I saw movement in the spot of trees and bushes where I heard the footstep getting closer.

I maintained my speed walking and didn't stop until I was in my office, with the door locked. I began shaking and quaking as the adrenaline wore off.

I called the security desk and asked for an escort to my car parked across the street in the lot. I nearly hugged the plain clothes security man who arrived.

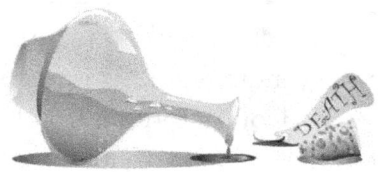

CHAPTER 19

I tossed and turned, flipped and flopped. My bed was the scene of emotional turmoil with the sheets and blankets twisted around my legs.

Every time I closed my eyes I felt Liam's kiss and how I responded to him. Sure, Mason and I were broke up, but I still felt guilty. Guilty over the kiss, over my not telling Liam straight up I was still emotionally involved with Mason. Okay, he seemed to have figured some of that out on his own, but still. Was I hedging my bets or was torturous indecision my new problem?

Then there was Mason. I kept replaying his hurt look when he saw Liam holding my hand and his guarded gaze from the door with his sister. What about Marisa? Had she talked to him yet?

Then I felt guilty for not focusing on Roderick Rogers' death. I didn't have a clue what to do next, and I was coming up with nothing of value from all my efforts. I was miserable.

I kicked at the covers that were imprisoning me until I was loose. I was getting frustrated and angry with my situation. I flipped on the bedside lamp and grabbed a notebook and the library book "Reward: Anthology of Unsolved Crimes of the Last Three Decades."

The reward part of the title was misleading because resolving these outstanding and high profile crimes might give you the reward of notoriety. But I suspected Mr. Rogers was more interested in finding the stolen loot or blackmailing the thieves. I couldn't tell from my cellphone photo where the bookmark might have been, so I scanned through the book.

I was quickly sucked into the various heists over the last few decades. There were several including: the Paris Diamond Heist with $107 million worth of jewelry stolen from a Harry Winston store, the Belgium Diamond Heist of $127 million (the world-record for a diamond heist), the Vestberga Robbery where helicopters were used to rob a Swedish cash service building and up to ten thieves got away, the French Bank Vault Robbery where $29 Million Euros was stolen and only one person was caught but the majority of the money was never recovered.

I was still wide awake and wasn't any closer to drifting off so I got up and made coffee and threw together some fruit and yogurt for breakfast. I sat at the dinner table and continued with the book.

I resumed with the Tucker Cross that was a recovered sunken gold cross encrusted with emeralds and was on display in a museum until it was discovered stolen and a replica sat in its place, then the serial bank robber nicknamed the Geezer Bandit by FBI after sixteen bank robberies throughout California who may have used special effects mask to appear older, the Gardner Museum Heist where two men posing as police officers got away with thirteen works of art worth around $500 million, then the Plymouth Mail Robbery where two gunmen dressed as police stole small bills en route to the Federal Reserve in a mail truck with a current value of the heist estimated at over $12 million dollars.

I was nearing the end of the book, finishing the fascinating DB Cooper case where a man hijacked an airliner and extorted $200,000 dollars for its release then parachuted from the plane never to be apprehended, when I turned to the next chapter and there it was... the David Marks Ponzi heist. Could that be the Mr. Marks that Rick Rogers asked me about?

The David Mark Ponzi Heist occurred twenty-five years ago, after police caught up with a ponzi scheme manager, all the sixty-five million dollars in the man's personal account that he had scammed from investors was gone and his personal assistant David Marks had disappeared without a trace. The Ponzi scheme manager went to prison but David Marks and the money was never found.

At first I wondered if Rick Rogers had been attempting to uncover DB Cooper like so many over the years had or maybe he had some ideas on the Geezer Bandit, but it now seemed clear he was looking into David Marks of the Ponzi scheme heist.

That would be tough because the photo of Marks was of a young man's driver's license who wouldn't look anything like that now. He probably altered his appearance besides aging.

I figured that Marks would have a lot to lose even though it's a cold case. The families of the bilked investors would jump at civillaw suits, his new identity would be revealed and his family, which he likely had started after all this time, would be shattered to discover what he had done and the secrets he kept. I didn't know if his current assets could be frozen or confiscated because of such an old crime, but no doubt the IRS would come after him for money owed!

Which meant David Marks would likely be a desperate man, especially if Rogers found him and was stupid enough to try to blackmail him. But, without my having access to Rogers' copy of the book or to his office to find any notes or research he may have done on Marks, there was no way of knowing if this was just a hobby or if he was onto something.

I finished my breakfast and got ready for work. I had backed out of my garage onto the road when I noticed Mason and an older gentleman standing in his driveway. They appeared to be in an argument from the red faces and crossed arms on both. Oh, I bet that was General Sheridan, Mason's father. The General stood ramrod straight, and he had the aura of a man who was used to being obeyed, unquestioningly.

Mason looked just as unbending and angry, which I had never seen before. I remembered Marisa saying the General had always been hard on Mason. It was interesting that in the six or seven months he had lived here, this was the first time I knew of that he visited his son. Families are the hardest.

I wanted to be there to lift Mason's spirits after his father left, but there was still too much unresolved between us. I crept my car along, watching the showdown between the two when Mason glanced my way. For a split second I saw sadness in his eyes. My heart went out to him and I realized this was likely embarrassing for him.

Then the General turned and looked at me, then he pointed and said something to Mason I didn't hear. Before I could zoom away, the General stalked over and was knocking on my car window.

In my defense, I was operating on maybe an hour's worth of sleep; I was getting nowhere in my exploration of Rogers' death and connection to the resort or myself; I felt guilty over Liam, and seemed to be pining for Mason. So you can see how the following uncharacteristic behavior exploded from me.

It was the bullish act of a stranger knocking on my window as if he was in charge that really set me off. I stopped in the middle of the street, put my car in park, grabbed by cell phone, and got out.

"Are you the reason my son thinks photography is a real job? Did you fill his head with nonsense?" His scarlet-with-rage face only inches from mine.

"Who do you think you are to be... " I ticked off fingers, "disturbing the peace this early in the morning, showing little respect for Mason or his neighbors, acting like you own the place, and fourth marching up to a woman who doesn't know who you are and pound on her car window like a brutish Neanderthal." I held up my phone and took several pictures.

"Don't talk to me in such tones. You need to learn some respect for your elders. No wonder you and my irresponsible son were together." He poked his index finger into my shoulder.

I stood on tiptoe and got closer to his face, yelling louder than I did at a football game, "I was raised that people had to earn respect and all you've earned is a phone call to the police for menacing."

I lifted my cell phone, "Yes, I have an emergency. I'm being harassed by a strange man outside my house. He blocked my car from leaving, pounded on my window, and is aggressive and belligerent." I supplied my address.

I hung up and glared at him, "The police are on their way and I plan to press charges, I'll be sure to contact the papers about an Air Force General's scary and menacing behavior."

Mason's father turned ghostly pale and stalked to his car. His tires screeched as he roared away. I turned to find Mason staring at me with his mouth open.

"I've never seen anybody stand up to the almighty General Sheridan like that. Did you really call the police on my father?" One side of his mouth lifted in a half smile.

"No, I called a pre-recorded inspirational message number. But he never needs to know that." I smiled in return.

Mason looked down at the asphalt, "I'm sorry he bushwhacked you like that. He was out of line."

"You don't apologize for him. The only one I want to

hear an apology from is him, and that's not just to me but to you as well." I meant it too. I still had my dander up, and I'd made up my mind.

"I saw the mention of you in that article in the paper. That Tiffany gal really doesn't know how to let anything go. Are you okay?" He was making eye contact now. His startlingly intense gaze snatched my breath.

"Thanks, I'm okay. I think. Mind if I ask what had your dad's tidy-whities twisted in such a bunch?" I leaned against my car door and crossed my ankles. I needed to calm down before driving, anyway.

He leaned against my car next to me, "He's been pressuring me to reenter the military, but this time the Air Force like he wanted me to do in the first place. He has been pulling strings and manipulating where he wants me, but I refuse to go back."

Wow, the man had no sense of boundaries and really was used to people jumping at his command. I couldn't imagine growing up with a parent who was so rigid and… well, devoid of any nurturing.

"I didn't know he was such a Napoleon. Actually, Napoleon wasn't entirely bad, maybe Attila the Hun." I joked and nudged him with my elbow.

"As a teen I swore he was insane and torturing me." He was serious.

I liked just talking again, being next to each other. But now that I had met his father, I knew where he got his stubbornness. Maybe we would only be friends and I would have to accept that.

He took a breath, "I know you're on your way to work, but I'd like for us to clear the air a bit. Do you think we can do that?" He put his hands up in surrender, "I promise not to set off your inner lioness."

"Actually talk rather than avoiding the taboo subject between us and just trying to win me back on your charms? I'd like that. But I'm crazy busy at the moment. It may be a day or two before I can give the time and attention this deserves." I didn't want him to think I was just brushing him off, and it was too soon to tell him about my looking into Rogers' death.

He took my hand and kissed it like the first time we met, "I look forward to talking."

Oh, how I missed him. A smile spread across my face and warmth from the top of my head to my toes.

I got to the office and had to force myself to think about something other than Mason and our brief meeting. I got a giant iced, blended mocha coffee to help stay awake. Now that I was at work, I was fighting to stay awake. I started in on my regular duties before I got into the Rogers case again.

It was about an hour and a half later when Liam knocked on my door. He didn't lean against the doorframe, but stood with a reserved air about him. He wore faded jeans, a polo shirt, and no cologne today. Things between us changed after last night. I hoped I hadn't hurt him, but honestly we barely knew each other. There was the nagging whisper insisting he only wanted a person in the London resort he offered that would perform MI5 small jobs like planting bugs in rooms.

I offered one of my professional smiles to help him feel comfortable without encouraging him. "Good morning, any news from Detective Lawrence?"

"I spoke to him briefly. All they know so far is the poison is organic, maybe from a flower or weed. The lab may take another week to identify the exact source. They think it may have been injected since the Medical Examiner found a small puncture on both Rogers and Peggy Faire. He hasn't any official persons of interest and I got the impression it may end up a cold case." His voice had lost its sparkle, along with his eyes.

I filed the information away in my mind. I didn't know much about poisonous plants other than Poinsettias must be kept away from pets. I could see another internet search in my future. But the injection aspect made this even harder.

I remembered during the cold war Russians would use the tip of an umbrella to inject radiation or Ricin into a person as they walked past and a few days later the person died. Not that I thought somebody used the umbrella trick or spies were involved, it was just a sinister way to kill. Rogers could be injected with the poison anywhere. Somebody might have followed Rogers into a bathroom and bumped into him, jabbed him with the needle. In a matter of minutes he's dead while driving. That just made this so much harder.

"Remember when I took photos of Rogers' office. Well, he had a book sitting out bookmarked," I showed him the photograph I took on my cell. "I found the book at the library and went through it. You'll never guess what I found."

He shrugged, so uncharacteristic of the Liam I had gotten to know. "I can't imagine. But I'll guess a clue of some sort."

"Mr. Marks is in the book." I said it in a *Tada* sort of way.

His eyebrows drew together then cleared, "Oh, the person Rogers asked you about. Who is this Mr. Marks then?"

I motioned for him to have a seat, but he remained standing. He didn't seem angry, just stiff and uncomfortable. He tucked his hands into his pockets making him appear unsure and even a little shy.

"He's a thief who took off with the ill-gotten gains from a Ponzi scheme while the guy who scammed the money from investors went to jail. There are rewards for some of the outstanding cases in the book which I figure is why Rogers probably had the book."

"So what're you thinking? He saw this thief while following the Sheriff and Commissioner around? Then why would he ask you if you had seen him?" He had progressed to standing just inside my doorway.

"Hmmm. Maybe he thought he saw Mr. Marks, but after a few decades couldn't be sure so asked me. Although I'd imagine David Marks would have a new name to elude the police."

"I don't know what you told him."

"I believe I told him I couldn't say anything, meaning I couldn't discuss guests or clients. I didn't even look for the name until yesterday."

"Maybe Rogers took that as you knew something but just couldn't reveal what you knew. So he wrote your name on the resort card and planned on getting you to talk somehow."

I looked at him like he was a genius. "That makes

sense. It clears the resort of any actual tie other than a coincidence and explains my name on the card when I barely spoke to him." I was so relieved. That had to be the answer.

Of course, there was still a killer who took two people's lives running around free. My excitement faded.

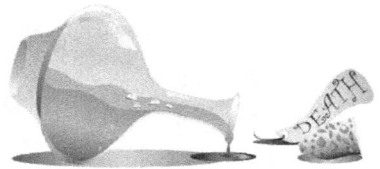

CHAPTER 20

"I'll have my lawyer turn over to the police what I found so far on the suspects. Maybe something there will help them find the killer."

"Including the Sheriff and Commissioner's illicit affair?" He cocked an eyebrow.

"I'll give a copy of the DVDs and our notes with times and let them figure it out, if Chad will let me that is." I couldn't imagine he would object.

"We never got anything on Donald Guy, did we?" He was shifting his weight, I could tell he wanted to be done with the case, and with me no doubt.

"Well, I did do some surveillance on him one night." I hoped he wouldn't need any further details.

"Oh, you didn't mention it before." He scrutinized me. His job must make him suspicious. "Staked out his flat or something?"

"Spoke to a neighbor, and he went to a bar so I had a few drinks and heard a little gossip. He sure as blazes has a temper from what I was told."

"A bar, you followed him to a bar?" His mouth dropped open and his eyebrows reached for the sky, "The file said he went to some stripper joint... you didn't..." He covered his gaping mouth with a hand.

"What if I did? I was only there for a half hour or so and I got some dirt on him. It was no big deal." I stopped while he chuckled, then he laughed out loud. "I think you're making a bigger deal out of this than... than it warrants." I crossed my arms.

"Did you get propositioned?" He asked between laughs.

"No, of course not." I may have tossed my hair and put my nose in the air at this point. *Really, the nerve!* At least the ice broke between us.

"You," he waved his hand up and down to indicate me, "didn't get propositioned in a strip joint - alone?"

"I was wearing my reserved work clothes, and I talked to a woman bartender. I didn't ask any of the patrons any questions." I wasn't stupid.

He wagged a finger at me, "You aren't telling something. That makes me want to find out even more. You might as well just tell me."

I let out a heavy sigh to cover my embarrassment, "I was offered a job which I turned down despite the ridiculous wage he promised I could get."

He stopped laughing, "At least he had taste. I have no doubt you could probably make that ridiculous wage if resort management loses its appeal."

"I don't intend to find out, ever."

He shook his head and forced the smile off his face. "What did you find out about Donald Guy?"

I filled Liam in on his being more likely to shoot a person than wait for poison to work.

"I actually stopped by because Ariya wanted me to remind you about the post wedding party at the in-law's house." He handed me a paper, "That's the address and the party will be going into the night so stop by anytime. I'll be there so if this is awkward I can explain to Ariya."

"No, I'll stop by for a little while. I'm due some time off so maybe I can leave a little early today and swing by." I couldn't look him in the face. It was awkward even though I didn't want it to be.

Liam left, and I caught Chad between meetings to give him my results of everything I found in the connection to the resort.

"So you don't think this was due to the Sheriff's affair?" He held his breath.

"I'm not a hundred percent positive, but I think his curiosity in an old cold case had him take a resort card and write my name on it. I can't prove it." Then I asked about turning over copies of the surveillance tapes to the police and letting them deal with the scandal.

"Oh, I like that. It's their job anyway and then you won't be in anymore trouble with Detective Lawrence."

I spent the next few hours getting the box of DVDs duplicated and returned the originals to security.

I couldn't let things go that easily though. I did an internet search on poisonous flowers and weeds. There were many flowers dangerous to dogs and cats. I was taking notes, so I wouldn't use any in planters around my home and hurt any neighborhood animals.

But for killing people, of course Foxglove and Wolf's

Bane, but I didn't realize Larkspur, Morning Glory, Lily of the Valley, Daffodil, Azalea, Hydrangea, and Oleander were so deadly.

It was very eye opening, but that didn't help me much either since flower gardens everywhere had these common flowers. Delores had Morning Glories outside her home and my Aunt Regina had both Hydrangea and Oleander in her garden. Even if one of my suspects had the flowers growing in their home, it wouldn't be a smoking gun. I finished my research and faced the task I was avoiding.

It was time I call Mr. Chalmers Esquire, "I have some resort surveillance recordings to turn over to the police that have the deceased Roderick Rogers on them. Plus some notes I took on suspects. I can drop them by your office if you like."

"That will be fine Miss LaMere. I wanted to let you know I spoke to the paper about the slanderous mention of you in the article. They were properly motivated to amend their ways and will print a retraction. I would look for that and save it, just for future reference."

Things were shaping up. Except two people were dead, and the killer was still free. That was the only thing that weighed on my mind.

My cell phone rang, Porsche.

"Hey girlfriend, what's up?" I was feeling a little more upbeat.

"Julie, Johan is in town. I'm meeting him for dinner and I thought you would like to say hi to him." Her voice was a little higher than usual.

"Sure, thank you for inviting me to dinner with you

guys." I didn't plan on spending more than a few minutes to say hello, but I had to give her a hard time. It's in the girlfriend rule book.

"I didn't…"

"Oh, it'll be so good to catch up with Johan, reminisce about catching a killer together. Fun times." She had to know I was joking.

"Woman, don't push your luck or there'll be another murder." Her voice was back to normal, and she sounded herself again.

"Are you nervous? I thought things were going well considering you're separated by the great Rocky Mountains." I dropped the joking and was serious.

"I don't know what to think. We've managed to see each other a few times, meeting midway. But this is the first time he's come all the way into town and I get the impression this is different." Her voice had crept higher.

"Are you afraid he'll break up with you?" Time to rip the bandage off, so to speak.

"I guess so. I don't know what's gotten into me Julie. I never let dates get this under my skin." She gave the most dejected sigh.

"All I can tell you is what I know. You will make it through whatever happens because you're strong. Johan isn't like any of your dates you've had before, so stop comparing them. All I care about is your happiness. That's what I know."

She gave me directions to a family owned Italian restaurant, and when to meet – in an hour, before we hung up. That left me just enough time to drop the box off at Mr. Chalmers' office. So I finished up for the day and locked up my office.

I took some time to explain how to Mr. Chalmers the notes went with the tapes for the times when Mr. Rogers was on the recordings. He took everything and said he would deliver tonight on his way home.

I made it to the restaurant with five minutes to spare and sat with Porsche waiting for Johan. I relaxed with some coffee while waiting.

I slapped Porsche's hand, "Stop biting your nails."

She glared at me. Finally, Johan walked up to the table. His sandy blonde hair was brushed back, his blue eyes warm and inviting, and he wore slacks and a button-down shirt. It was the first time I saw him without bulky sweaters and parkas. He had broad shoulders and was trim. He hadn't changed much, still the Nordic rugged good looks.

He barely noticed I was present as he stood there looking at Porsche, his blue eyes speaking for him. I cleared my throat.

"Oh Miss LaMere, I didn't see you there." I forgot about his butterscotch and caramel voice, sweet and warm with a touch of salt.

"I noticed. Don't worry I won't be the third wheel for long."

He sat as close as he could get to Porsche. I know they didn't get to spend much time together, but he barely noticed there was a whole wide world around him. I was about to just slip away and leave them alone when Porsche finally remembered I was there.

"Did I tell you that Julie is working another murder?"

Well that was one guaranteed way to get his attention! Sure enough, he dragged his gaze away from Porsche long enough to give me a *what is this I hear young lady?* look.

"Yeah, it's no big deal. How is Vail? Weather warming up?" I tried to redirect away from me.

"Don't change the subject. You better tell me what's going on."

Why? So he could call the local police and tell them I was curious and they might want to reign me in? I don't think so, mister.

"I was the first one the detective questioned, thank you very much. Plus a local reporter insinuated I was involved with a murder because my name and resort's card was found on the man's body." I guess I was a little defensive.

"Would you feel better if you had an ally on the force?" His question took me by surprise.

"Um, I guess so. But you're the only cop I know who listens to me." I didn't finish. What was he hinting at?

He shifted in his chair, "I wanted to tell Porsche first, but I'm here interviewing for a position as Detective on the city force. I don't know what my chances are, but I have to try."

Porsche threw her arms around his neck. When she finally let go her eyes were moist. Johan had changed her into a sentimental and tenderhearted girl. He better not hurt her.

We peppered him with questions. He didn't know much other than what the job posting said, but he was hoping his experience on homicide and prior with drug cartel investigations would tip the scale in his favor.

"Enough about the job since I know so little about it. What's this murder you're connected to?"

"Have you ever seen the reality television show Real Investigators?"

"Sure, it's my guilty pleasure since it isn't hard core investigations like I'm involved in."

"Well, Rick Rogers on the show was poisoned and he had a Colorado Springs Resort card with my name written on it in his pocket when he died in traffic causing an accident."

I explained what I found in trying to clear the resort from any connection.

"My theory is he was trying to follow up on an old cold case about David Marks who stole ponzi scheme money. I figure he thought maybe I knew the name and that's why he wrote my name on a resort card." I tried to make it all sound so yesterday's news, nothing to see hear, and especially nothing to tattle to Detective Lawrence.

"Hmmm, I think I remember that old case. There are a number of amateurs who have become obsessed over that and the DB Cooper case." He rubbed his jaw.

"Yeah, it wouldn't be easy because the man probably changed his name, with that kind of money he could have changed his appearance too." I was feeling like I had stayed too long and wanted to let them have time together.

"You can easily change your hair, even contacts for eye color, lose or gain weight, but he had two things you can't change easily. This was in a class I took ages ago so most books and such don't have this information. He had a tattoo of a diamond on his bicep."

Porsche had stopped dabbing her eyes and joined in, "But can't you get tattoos removed now?"

"Laser removal of tattoos can cause scaring and burns, so there is a chance there is proof there had been a tattoo. As a law enforcement professional that is one of the things I would look for."

"You said two things, what's the other?"

"He had a crooked pinky finger from a break that didn't set and heal properly as a kid. If he had gotten that corrected, even as an adult, xrays would still show it. Oh, and he studied piano and played well, but that isn't very unique."

We chatted for a little longer and then I got out of their way so they could make lovey eyes at each other. I wasn't sure what to make of the news Larson was interviewing for the local police force. There was a part of me that feared Detective Armstrong's negative view of me might influence Johan rather than the other way around.

I was putting off attending the Garrett day-after-wedding party. It was kind of Ariya to invite me but I wasn't family or even a friend and Ariya hadn't been subtle in trying to convince me to get together with her brother. Liam's presence would make it awkward.

But if I was going, I had better just get it over with.

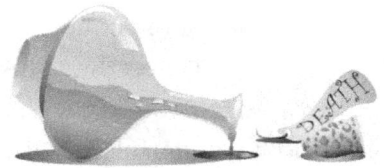

CHAPTER 21

I followed the directions Liam had left me. Landon Garrett's house, or should I say property, was in a hidden pocket. Large lots that maintained a more rural feel with old-growth trees and city maintained dirt roads that were literally just off a main street and next to a large acreage of natural parkland. Most people never knew these little islands of expensive homes that had the best of both worlds existed.

The long driveway, lined with aspens and a variety of other trees, had a multitude of cars parked along the sides. This was a big party. Maybe I could make an appearance and in a half hour leave with everyone satisfied. It wouldn't be as awkward as I feared. I found a spot and parallel parked my economy car between a Lexus and an Audi. Not awkward at all.

I was greeted at the door by Landon's wife who I only knew was diabetic and had the special mini-cake at the reception. She looked like a young and energetic fifty something with short blonde hair going white and a big generous smile.

"I'm Lillian," her sophisticated voice gushed as she welcomed me. "I'm so glad you joined us, Ariya will be delighted. You helped us out in a tight spot accommodating the wedding on such short notice." She laid a hand on my arm, friendly as could be. She was a *toucher*, you know the type, have to touch you as they talk to you. "I've told all my friends how wonderful you are so you should be getting plenty of business my dear." She smiled a toothy grin. "Oh and thank you for arranging a special cake at the reception. I know that's a bother." She took my arm in hers and escorted me into her small mansion.

"I don't know how you do it, I couldn't give myself insulin. I nearly faint at needles." I confessed. I was a wimp.

"It's been twenty years of shots for me, I still hate it. But I had to suck it up and learn to cope with it." She squeezed my arm. "Things have changed over the years, now you get everything pre-packaged and don't have to worry about the syringes much anymore."

At that moment Liam appeared, "Lillian, there is a brandy shortage and Landon sent me in search of you. I guess you know where his stash is."

Lillian look at me with an apology in her eyes.

"Don't worry about me, I'm fine." Other than being left alone with the person I wanted to avoid the most. *No problem.*

Lillian gave me an apologetic smile and scurried off to avert a Brandy shortage crisis. Liam motioned me into the formal living room that looked like a photo out of a better living magazine. It reeked of a professional decorator from its coordinated blues and silver with dark cherry wood accents. The paintings were actual oils, not prints, in sleek frames. They weren't boring mountains or hunting scenes either; the paintings were abstract with lots of white space and splashes of color.

The only personal touch was the bank of family photos tastefully arranged on several shelves of the bookcase that had maybe ten books on display. I walked over to gaze at the photos to appear cool and collected with Liam standing there.

"It doesn't have to be uncomfortable, we're adults, and we were honest with each other. I have no regrets."

"I know that in my head, but I still feel I hurt you or maybe let things go too long." It came out before I could check my filters on what I was saying. I was looking over the photos of Landon with Lillian and Jason. There were photos of travel around the world, but the most interesting was of a camping trip and around a piano.

My hand took a photo in a bold silver frame with fine etching from the shelf. It was the only photo with everyone in casual shorts and tank tops or t-shirts. Jason was probably eight years old. They were posed for the picture, each holding up a fish they had caught, Jason holding up a twelve inch trout proudly. I was surprised to notice a tattoo on Landon's arm after just talking to Johan about a diamond one.

But Landon's was of a crown with multifaceted gems set among ornate gold scroll work. That said a lot about the man I thought.

"Believe it or not, it isn't the first time I've been rejected. Although, you'll be hard to forget."

I sat the photo back on the shelf, "I don't think you're being completely honest. I bet you could have all the dates you want back in London. I even bet you've broken a few hearts yourself." I gave a half smile to show I was teasing him. Okay, maybe I wasn't teasing after all.

"I can't speak to the breaking hearts without sounding egotistical, but I might turn down more dates than I divulged." He dropped his eyes to study the carpet. "I thought I needed all the help I could get to persuade you to look at me as more than a guest in your resort or as a 'gal in every port' man."

I changed the subject, "How about you show me where the party is and we can let that confession drop."

He took my arm and led me through the house to the French doors that opened up onto a landscaped backyard that must have been in Better Homes and Gardens at some point. There was a stamped concrete patio with a river stone faced grilling station that would have a professional chef jealous including a bar fridge, stovetop, and warming oven. But the jaw dropping feature was the stucco pizza oven.

There was wide open lawn with bronze statues of children playing or fishing, even a statue of a young lady seemingly suspended in air on a swing placed among flowers or decorative bushes. There was an actual running fountain depicting children holding the urns that splashed water into the basin. All along the high wood privacy fence was an elaborate flower garden with the spring Tulips, Daffodils, and Irises blooming. It was a showpiece meant to impress.

Ariya rushed over and gave me a big hug, "I'm so glad you came. We have food left from lunch and haven't started on dinner yet."

Maybe I could stay long enough to eat something; since I didn't stick around with Porsche long enough to order anything and I had skipped even a granola bar for breakfast. I was rather hungry now that she mentioned it. She fixed me up with items in the warming oven, such leftovers as grilled Salmon with peppers and onions with a side of asparagus. Ariya brought me some of the Brandy too. It was the best leftovers ever.

Between Ariya, Liam, and Lillian I wasn't alone for more than a minute or two even while I devoured my meal. I decided the after dinner Brandy was pretty good too. *Like I would actually know!* Then there was leftover wedding cake that was actually yummy.

I was stuffed like a big turkey in November, moving was uncomfortable. But I forced myself to get up and move around or I would fall asleep, probably drool or embarrass myself another way. So I carried dishes to the sink in the spacious kitchen. I walked the yard to work off some of the food. Lillian joined me and I received a running commentary on her plans for what flowers were strategically placed where and why and how it would change from spring through to fall with ever-blooming flowers of one variety or another.

I was a simple flower person, give me Petunias and Marigolds that are hardy and bloom all season and I'm done. None of this elaborate planning of what each flower's schedule is and where to place it. I remember falling in love with Lilacs to find out they only bloomed for a few weeks each year and I felt so cheated. Although I admit the bank of Tulips, Daffodils, and Irises were lovely.

We made the entire circuit of the yard and I knew more than I ever wanted to about Lillian's hobby. I was impressed since my first impression was that a professional landscape artist must have been hired. But it was all Mrs. Garrett.

"Thank you for allowing me to bring my own flowers in for the rehearsal dinner centerpieces. I'm so tickled with how my flowers have turned out I wanted to show them off. Besides, we needed some colors other than red and white." She smiled, but it was the first hint she hadn't been altogether pleased with the wedding.

"If I had such a green thumb, I would want to show it off too. Glad it all went so smoothly." But there was something forming in the back of my mind. Something to do with Rogers' murder and I needed to do some research of my own. Maybe I wasn't done with my questions on the case after all.

I was suddenly eager to leave. I said my goodbyes to Ariya and Lillian. Liam said he would stop by tomorrow when he checked out to say his goodbye, which was a relief. I knew I was delaying the inevitable stiff and uncomfortable scene, but I would deal with that tomorrow.

I was out the door and took off in my car back to the resort.

CHAPTER 22

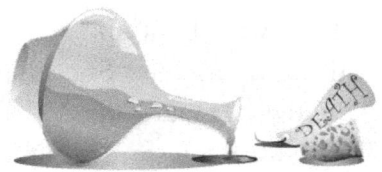

On the drive back to my office I reviewed my one and only meeting with Rogers. I hadn't been aware of who David Marks was or his tattoo until recently. What was formulating in my mind was a real long shot.

I didn't want to share it with anyone because they may think my imagination was running wild. People might point to my involvement in investigating three separate incidents of multiple murders as making me look for killers everywhere.

I jogged from the parking lot into the resort, unlocked my office door and turned my computer on. I drummed my fingers waiting for everything to finish loading.

This morning Liam and I had surmised that Rick Rogers probably saw what he thought was the thief from the Ponzi scheme heist and asked me. But I had dropped it there feeling the resort, and myself were absolved from his death. I didn't look at our suspects as potential David Marks.

First, I did an internet search for David Marks. I switched to images and finally found a photo of the tattoo. Just as Johan had said, it was of a single diamond, side view showing the facets. Rather basic line drawing except for some subtle ice blue shading.

I wish I had known about the tattoo when I was checking out Mike Hammond, Sheriff Morrison and Donald Guy. Although, Donald the Menace seemed all wrong to be David Marks wearing suits and playing a long con. Since I had seen Vincent Vanders in his shorts and polo shirt with no evidence of ink or removal scaring, so I dismissed him. I tried a Google search on each of the others.

Hammond and the Sheriff had plenty of photos since they were in the public eye. There seemed to be a few tattoos on Hammond but none showed more than a little ink peeking from the edge of a short-sleeve shirt. The same results with the Sheriff. There was nothing on Donald Guy, again.

I sat and thought back to my meeting with Mr. Rogers, what I had been doing. Logically, it was probably somebody I saw, maybe even interacted with for Rogers to ask me, not a desk clerk or a valet, or any number of other people. I had passed several people as I showed Ariya around, spoken to a few of them as well.

I grabbed the library book on unsolved heists and opened to the page on David Marks. There wasn't any mention of the tattoo, but it gave a website address that covered theories and clues. I typed in the webpage address and found photos of Mr. Marks and his tattoo.

I stared at his face, the basic bone structure doesn't

change easily. My crazy theory might not be such a stretch. The rest of the website tracked theories of where David Marks might have escaped to.

Several people figured that Marks had gotten out of the country since he had roughly a twenty-four-hour head start before the police put a lock down on the accounts only to find Marks had drained the accounts. There was a list of countries with no extradition treaty with the U.S. Others figured he ditched his car, maybe had a new identity waiting for the right moment, and drove to the west coast of Mexico in a cheap car he got for cash.

A knock on the door interrupted my reverie; I looked up to find one of our uniformed security guys with his walkie talkie.

"Ms. LaMere, we got somebody at the Ballroom saying they left something there yesterday at the wedding."

"Have they checked Lost and Found?"

"He claims he checked with them and no luck. He wants let into the space to look around."

"I'm guessing you can't do it for him and you want me to."

His radio squawked, "We got a shoplifter coming your way through the lobby. Two teens, male and female." And the uniformed security man was gone at a run.

Sure, I'll walk all the way across the lake and over to the Ball-room on my day off to make a customer happy.

A little voice somewhere in my head whispered there was something strange about this. The core of my gut turned ice cold. I grabbed my key set for the ballroom...

and my pepper spray that Mason had convinced me to carry when we first met.

I walked through the lobby with security taking two teens away to call parents about the shoplifting, and out the back doors through the Lake Patio seating. I hesitated a few moments before the walkway across the lake, squared my shoulders, and took a deep breath to calm my nerves that this was a bad idea. *A terrible idea.*

I tucked the pepper spray into my pants pocket and forced my feet to move. Each step across the walkway was a struggle, my spidey senses were screaming to turn back. The logical part of my brain calmly reassured that I was simply too involved in murder and the darker side of human nature and it was creating paranoia.

But then again, just because you're paranoid…

I finally stepped onto the concrete sidewalk on the other side of the lake and stopped, rooted in place. My feet only wanted to turn around and run.

"Excuse me miss, can I get past you?" A woman's voice behind me asked. I nearly jumped out of my skin.

I was being foolish. I walked on and hoped the woman didn't realize I worked here. I was standing at the Ballroom building's door looking around for the man who had to get in to find whatever was left behind. *It'll probably be something ridiculous, like his wife's favorite mascara.*

My arm was grabbed in a crushing grip I instinctively tried to break away from but couldn't.

"Don't fight this." Landon Garrett's gruff voice said next to my ear. "We're going to walk to the side of the building over here and talk."

Did he think I was stupid? I wasn't happy to have this

confirmation that my wild theory was apparently on the nose. But, I wasn't going to give him confirmation I knew he was the long lost David Marks of the Ponzi Heist.

"You wouldn't let that sleazy PI's death go." He snarled and his face transformed into an angry monster's.

"Sir, that is all in the past. The Resort is cleared of all but a cursory connection to him and that's all I was tasked to do, keep the Resort away from his death." His grip on my arm increased. "If you're concerned about our reputation, it's safe."

"Your little act isn't working Julienne. I've followed your progress from the beginning as Liam and Ariya would talk. I knew he was holding back, and it had to be because you were uncovering Rogers' information." He began shoving me to the side of the Ballroom building no matter how much I dug my pumps in.

He had a hold of my arm with the hand closest to my pepper spray and the other hand couldn't reach around and get the spray out at the odd angle. *Crap, double crap.*

"Liam's job has trained him to be tight-lipped you know." My voice was beginning to show hints of panic. My brain was trying to come up with logic to stall him so somebody would walk past and scare him away.

"You mean his desk job with some import export company? You'll have to do better than that." He wrenched my arm.,

Great, he didn't tell father-in-law he was MI5. Which, I'm guessing he would have panicked at that news thinking his game was up earlier and maybe even have hurt Ariya. But, I thought Liam said Mr. Garrett wasn't comfortable with his job, or was that just an excuse to explain why he wanted to spent time with me?

"As soon as Liam said you looked over the family photos and I found the camping trip photo out of alignment, I knew you figured it out."

If I was going to keep him talking, I might have to drop the innocent act. Besides, I didn't have anything logical left as a stall. He shoved me via my arm again.

"Sure, it was the only time in all the photos you seemed casual and enjoying yourselves."

"Don't pretend you didn't see the tattoo."

"Yes, I saw your tattoo. I never understood the appeal myself. I wondered if it was a youthful symbol of how you saw yourself, maybe a college graduation's vision of being at the top of your career field." I jerked my arm and tried to pry his fingers off with my free hand. "You're hurting me, let go."

His grip seemed unbreakable. I couldn't get to my pepper spray. I had nothing to grab and beat him with, nothing to brace my legs against to stop his shoving me to the side of the building. I suspected he had one of his wife's diabetic syringes loaded with a distilled poisonous flower tincture. His wife grew plenty of Daffodils and I found in the research they are toxic for pets and in large doses deadly for people.

"I saw that parasite Rogers talking to you after you initially showed us around. Did he tell you he recognized me?"

"No, he asked me about a Mr. Marks. I told him I didn't know any guest by that name. He left then. I swear. I don't know any Mr. Marks." Which was true in the strictest sense, but Rogers' blackmail attempt had him paranoid and thinking everyone knew who he was.

"You talked to that money grasping assistant of Roger's, that Peggy. She told you, I know she did. Liam said once she knew who you were she was nicer. Even the detective thought you and Peggy were up to something." He snarled in my face.

So, Peggy Faire attempted to blackmail the Ponzi Scheme Heist thief. I would bet she thought the Sheriff or another client killed Rogers and she could extort a small fortune from Marks for herself.

"Sir, she didn't tell me anything. I barely got information on his clients he was working on, which led to a number of people who had motives to kill him." Since Liam had been fairly quiet about all the details in my investigation, I hoped he hadn't shared how I got photos and the client files. He might think I knew more from those than I did.

"Excuse me, is there a problem here?" Mason stood about twelve feet away with a cautious look on his face. I didn't know what forces in the universe were at work, but I was overjoyed to see him. But I needed to warn him it was dangerous, and more serious than it looked.

"Get rid of him." Landon Garrett, or David Marks, growled.

"Sir, thanks for your concern." The vise grip on my arm tightened, and I sucked in my breath, "but I'm just having an anxiety attack and he's helping me." My arm was going numb from lack of blood flow.

Mason nodded. He got the message that this was a

dire predicament. Without another word he turned and walked the opposite direction.

Landon Garrett didn't wait but a few seconds and shoved me again toward the side of building again. I heard what had to be Mason rush up behind us and heard him take a breath. I felt Landon's arm receive a slam that broke his grip on me. I scrambled away from the struggle and fumbled for the pepper spray with my numb fingers. The canister dropped to the ground, and I snatched it up with my good hand.

I planned to spray Landon in the eyes and shorten the fight. But, I got the pepper spray and straightened just in time to witness Mason deliver a flying roundhouse kick to Landon's solar plexus that had him on the ground wheezing for air.

Before either of us could move, Landon took out a gun. Here I was expecting a poisonous syringe from his wife's old diabetic supplies. Maybe he didn't want my murder to be connected to Rogers' or Peggy's.

He had the gun pointed at Mason. But he took his eyes off me, and I was long past fear and anger was surging up. I eased the pepper spray up slowly to not draw attention. He glanced my way when a full blast hit him in the face.

"Hit the dirt." Mason yelled.

I didn't take the time to think, I just dropped as fast as I could and rolled away.

Landon was waving the gun around while attempting to rub the pepper spray off. In another few seconds he was cursing and yelling.

Mason had crawled over to where I stopped rolling

against the Ballroom locked doors. I reached up and unlocked the doors and we bolted inside and locked the door behind us.

Landon Garrett turned towards the door and squinted through red swollen eyes and raised his gun. *Oh crap, he could see us through the door.* Mason grabbed my hand, and we ran away from the door into the cavernous dark space.

We witnessed security surround Landon and wrestle him to the ground. Mason held me for a long time, smoothing my hair.

With my face buried in his shoulder and enveloped in his fresh smelling aftershave I asked, "How did you know I was in trouble?"

"I was sitting on the Lake Patio, hoping to ask you to dinner for our talk when I saw you walk out and slip the pepper spray in your pocket. I could tell you were nervous about something. So I ran around the north side of the lake keeping you in sight the best I could."

Coincidence? I like to believe something in the universe was looking out for me and Mason was tuned in.

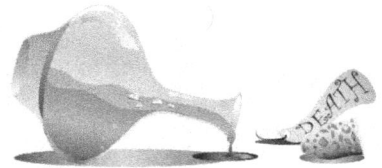

CHAPTER 23

*I*t was two days after Landon Garrett, formerly David Marks, was arrested for two counts of murder and attempted murder. His big mistake was resorting to killing to solve his problem with Roderick Rogers because he feared being exposed on the television show "Real Investigators."

Sheriff Leland Morrison and County Commissioner Shannon Gage were officially under investigation by the Department of Justice. It hadn't taken Detective Lawrence long to jump on the tapes and blow the whistle. I figure he owed me, but he would never admit that. Johan's interview went well. He and Porsche were anxiously awaiting news on whether or not he got the job. It would be nice to have Johan here for Porsche and my sake.

Mason and I were finally getting our talk. I wore long sleeves to cover the bruises on my arm from Garrett. We faced each other in a family owned Italian restaurant with a half-eaten pizza between us and my second glass of wine, his third. His wavy hair was tempting me to run my fingers through it and his blue eyes were soaking me in.

Now that it was finally time to hash out his posing as other women's boyfriend as a cover for doing bodyguard work, he was tongue-tied. I was too. I didn't want to ruin this détente, but we had to face the lurking elephant in the room, eventually.

I cleared my throat. "I met your sister a few days ago. Marisa. We had a nice chat." I figure if she talked to him about our situation then this was the easiest way to broach the topic.

He avoided my eyes and took several gulps from his wine. I tensed for what may come next.

"Marisa likes you a lot, at the moment, probably more than she likes me." A slight smile quirked one side of his mouth and then faded. "She umm, she really let me have it and blasted through my excuses."

I didn't know what to say. Should I explain our talk, tell him I never meant for her to be harsh, or some mixture of the two? Instead, I sat there, my mouth as dry as if we were in the Sahara desert in the middle of summer... at noon... with no shade or water. I squirmed in my chair and my feet were bouncing under the table.

"But she got me to understand your perspective by throwing in my face, repeatedly, how I felt when I saw that man holding your hand."

I opened my mouth to explain Liam, but he held up his hand, "Let me explain. Even if you told me it was nothing, or innocent, I still felt my gut twist into a knot as if I'd been sucker punched. She forced me to look at all the pictures that circulated during my last bodyguard job. She made me look at them as if it was you and that man I saw you with and pushed me relentlessly on how would I feel then?"

He ran a hand through his hair, drained his wine, and tore a paper napkin to shreds all without looking me in the eyes yet. "Then she told me how even your Aunt Regina, who I thought liked me, called you to break the news I was with somebody else. She kept pushing like my drill sergeant in boot camp, she was relentless."

I felt like I should say something, but my throat had closed down. I felt words die before they even reached my tonsils. *Just breathe LaMere, just breathe.*

"What I'm trying to say is," he shifted in his seat some, then finally lifted his gaze to look at me. "I apologize for being an ass, for not putting myself in your place sooner, and especially for ever saying you were overreacting. Can you forgive me?"

Tears sprang into my eyes instantaneously. That was all I had ever wanted.

"Don't worry, I won't pose as a boyfriend again. Any bodyguard jobs will be with male clients only." His eyes were bright with emotion.

I would have been happy with just not pretending to be their boyfriend, but I wasn't going to share that now. This was a far more reassuring solution for me.

I was still having trouble with my voice so it came out a deep croak, "I forgive you. But, what about you avoiding my father, what was that about?"

He turned a lovely shade of pink. "If I met your father, well you would then expect to meet my…" his voice trailed off.

I sucked in my breath as understanding dawned on me. "Your parents, including your father! You were afraid of my meeting your father." I shrugged a shoulder, "I guess I can understand that having met him now." Talk about your family drama. The great Santini and General Sheridan seemed to have a lot in common.

He reached over and took my hand in his, "Does this mean we can patch things up between us? I'm not too late am I? Some handsome Brit hasn't swept you off your feet and promised to show you Europe while I was being so pig-headed?"

Liam and I had parted friends, I think. He was busy consoling Ariya in the aftermath; reassuring her that her new husband was a good guy despite who his father happened to be.

"No, you're not too late. I'd like to give us an honest chance." I squeezed his hand. "Tell Marissa I owe her and hope to never piss her off."

He raised my hand to his lips in his classic move from when we first met and I melted under his gaze. Then my cell phone buzzed. I glanced to see who it was, planning on ignoring it.

"It's Chad, I should see if there's an emergency." He nodded. After a few short minutes I hung up.

"He has assigned me to receive extra duty training with the security department. He thinks I would be a natural at it."

Mason poured the few remaining ounces of wine from the bottle into his glass and we toasted to my new additional duty.

Imagine little ole me in security! I rather liked the idea.

AFTERWORD

Thank you for reading!

Dear Reader,

I hope you enjoyed SPIKED: Resort to Murder Mystery #3. I really enjoyed writing the characters of Julienne, Liam, Porsche, Mason, and the rest of the gang! I hope you enjoyed reading about their adventures, and hope you are looking forward to the next book, ARROWED.

Finally, I need to ask you a favor. If you're so inclined, I'd love a review of SPIKED. Whether you loved it or hated it - I'd just enjoy your feedback. Reviews can be tough to come by these days. You, the reader, have the power now to make or break a book.

Also, feel free to contact me at mysterysuspense1@gmail.com if you have spotted any typos that have escaped my editor and proofreader's attention. Subscribe to my newsletter for exclusive content and specials: http://eepurl.com/c2DgfT

Thank you for reading SPIKED and spending time with me.

In gratitude,
Avery Daniels

ABOUT THE AUTHOR

Avery Daniels was born and raised in Colorado, graduated from college with a degree in business administration, and has worked in fortune 500 companies and Department of Defense her entire life. Her most eventful job was apartment management for 352 units. She still resides in Colorado with two brother black cats as her spirited companions. She volunteers for a cat shelter, enjoys scrapbooking and card making, photography, and painting in watercolor and acrylic. She inherited a love for reading from her mother and grandmother and grew up talking about books at the dinner table.

Signup for exclusives http://eepurl.com/c2DgfT
Website: www.Avery-Daniels.com
Goodreads: www.goodreads.com/Avery-Daniels
Facebook: facebook.com/AveryDanielsAuthor
BookBub: www.bookbub.com/authors/avery-daniels

Next in Resort to Murder Mysteries is Arrowed.